Badlands

Other titles from Miami University Press

Badlands

By Cynthia Reeves

Miami University Press
Oxford, Ohio

Library of Congress Cataloguing-in-Publication Data

Reeves, Cynthia.
Badlands / by Cynthia Reeves.
p. cm.
A novella.
1. Breast—Cancer—Patients—Fiction. 2. Cancer—Psycho-
logical aspects—Fiction. 3. Married people—Fiction.
I. Title.
PS3618.E444B33 2007
811'.6--dc22
ISBN 978-1-4243-3108-6 (paperback)
ISBN 978-1-4243-3109-3 (cloth)

Grateful acknowledgement is made for permission to reprint
or adapt portions of material from:

"'My Soul Is a Light Housekeeper,'" from THE PROB-
ABLE WORLD by Lawrence Raab, copyright © 2000 by
Lawrence Raab. Used by permission of Penguin, a division
of Penguin Group (USA) Inc.

VOICES OF WOUNDED KNEE by William S. E. Coleman by permission of the University of Nebraska Press.
Copyright © 2000 by the University of Nebraska Press.

WEST, THE by GEOFFREY WARD. Copyright © 1996
by The West Book Project, Inc. By permission of LITTLE,
BROWN & COMPANY.

COYOTE STORIES by Mourning Dove by permission of
the University of Nebraska Press. Copyright © 1990 by the
University of Nebraska Press.

Cover painting by Rick A. Robbins
"White Buffalo," 1988
48" x 48" oil on canvas & cheesecloth
http://home.comcast.net/~rick1216/

For my family
Douglas, Elizabeth, and Christopher Reeves
and for my friend
Barbara, in loving memory

> . . . *Imagine, love,*
> *the tedium of this watch. On almost every day*
> *nothing happens. And isn't it wrong to yearn*
> *for a great storm just to feel important?*
> *. . . Imagine you could have seen that side of me*
> *at the beginning, when we walked*
> *for hours along the shore, and you were so certain*
> *I was yours just because you loved me.*

–Lawrence Raab
"'My Soul Is a Light Housekeeper'"

> *There were about four hundred people in Big Foot's band.*
> *There were 126 men, counting boys. Of the victims there were*
> *164 bodies buried at Wounded Knee. There were about one*
> *hundred survivors. The rest were not accounted for. They must*
> *have died in the prairie. Some of the bodies were found in Bad*
> *River, considerably more than one hundred miles away. Some*
> *of the wounded girls got back to the Cheyenne River still further*
> *away, but they afterwards died of their wounds and exposure.*

–Dr. Melvin R. Gilmore
"The Truth of the Wounded Knee Massacre"

Badlands

1

The weight of her dream: in the Badlands, sunburned prairie and windworn stone leach what little they require from the sky: moisture, oxygen, the fluid blue of heaven. Inside the canvas tent pitched in the Oligocene fossil beds, Caroline scrapes each shallow layer of thirty million years from rock and earth and grass root scabs, searching for—what, exactly? All around her is a vast graveyard, of titanothere and bison, the petrified remains of Paleo-Americans, the underbelly of an ancient sea.

Ces mauvaises terres que je dois traverser, she thinks, feeling safe within the confines of the weather-beaten tent. These bad lands that I must cross.

A lump of milky chalcedony emerges slowly from the earth. She pries the stone from the dirt with her fingers, breaks it open on an exposed outcropping of chert veined with charcoal, and studies the interior bloom of flame-colored agate: concentric circles of amber, gold, burnt umber. The rings fold and flow like liquid, heat emanates from the core through her skin, she is lost in the fire.

Professor Dietrich raps the metal blade of her trowel with his. —No time for daydreaming, he says. He taps her trowel again and lifts her chin with the sharp tip of his own shovel, leaving a pinprick of blood. It beads, it boils, and she wakes to Daniel's body cupped around her.

Her spine is on fire. She visualizes water, ice, snow, smothering her body, dousing the flames. This will pass, this will pass, she murmurs to herself, a mantra to dull the pain. She breathes deeply in and out. She hesitates one moment more, presses the button on her morphine pump, and waits.

§

Daniel reaches in his sleep for Caroline, her missing breast.

§

Daniel's chest palpitates against her back, one quick beat for each of his shallow inhalations. How would I know if he were having a heart attack? she wonders. Beat....beat....beat. His heart so sure of itself. Beat..beat..beat. This quickening: is it just another of my hallucinations? or maybe he's dreaming of something that revs his heart? of the Malaysian cashier, the one whose thick black hair falls to her waist, the one he favors at the grocery check-out? He thinks I don't notice. What he doesn't realize is that it doesn't matter anymore. It's been a long time, too long, since we were allowed... what was it the oncologist told him months ago?

No jogging, no lifting, no sex. Her spine might break.

They think I don't hear them. And so what if I break?

She pictures her shattered body scattered across the white sheet, Daniel naked and frantically gluing the pieces together, an enormous bottle of Elmer's glue in his hands. She giggles, swallows her mirth, but her laughter erases him, and all that is left is heat radiating from his skin into hers, his disembodied arm covering her arms, and the pulse of his heart against her back. Beat...beat....beat. Slowing down now, his heart searches for its customary rhythm, the normal rhythm it counts its days by.

I could make love simply to his beating heart. No, that wouldn't do. Besides, there's the matter of my body. Could he stand to look at it now? Well, if he were only heart, he wouldn't see my bald head, the scar that passes for my right breast, that thing growing from my navel. I will die, I am dying, I have died, and this is how he compensates. Find someone else, dear, your heart betrays you.

—Dietrich, she calls.

Dietrich's face looms, his black eyes fixed on a hollow, ivory tube he rolls between his thumb and forefinger. Deep squint lines fan out across his temples and the rounded flesh of his cheeks. He stands near a dusty plastic tent window, his white shirt streaked with dirt, his jeans worn gray at both knees, his legs permanently bowed from years of squatting in earthen trenches just like the one in which Caroline finds them now. He is close enough for her to smell his wintergreen breath and touch the wiry, gray hairs protruding from his nose.

—Clay pipe, he says, and scrapes some black flecks from its surface with his fingernail. —Probably Sioux. Nothing more. He places the pipe to his lips, blows, and in a single moment, eradicates a century's ash. Then he tosses it back to her.

She catches the pipe just before it hits the ground. Holding it up to the light, she examines the slight symmetrical flaring at its head and base, features that had made her think it was a bone from a human finger. —But these others are bones, definitely bones.

—Not human. Animal. Buffalo, or more precisely, bison. Coyote. Pheasant.

He points to a small pile of bones she has spent the week unearthing with razor blades and paintbrushes, her bare hands. —This site suggests a large fire pit, coyote roasting on a spit, bison boiling in iron vats, men sharing a post-supper smoke.

—I understand Sioux culture.

—Garbage, dear girl. Sioux garbage. He is leaning too close; his arm brushes her high ponytail.

Move, she thinks, now. But she cannot move.

—We're after far more than this. He waves his hand over the bones like a magician, and the pile disappears. —You can't leave. I need you here.

—What about Daniel? What about the children?

—Marriage? You're twenty-two, for God's sake. Children? I'm offering you a chance to discover the first Americans. Dear girl, I'm offering you Eden.

—Fire pits and shards of clay pipes? She shakes her head. —You'd sacrifice everything for the slim chance of discovery? Here?

He tucks a loose strand of hair behind her ear. —I already have.

She fingers through the fabric of her jeans the amber trinket hidden in her pocket, the one Dietrich had worn on a slender silver necklace ever since she had known him, the one she had stolen as his punishment.

What did her professor know of love?

2

All along the gash of Wounded Knee Creek lies the limitless map of the Dakotas. The slash of frozen creek snakes through a grid winnowing away to forever. For a moment, Caroline understands that the universe is a tumbling infinity of cubes, everything at once disordered and controlled, the universe composed of broken cubes, perennial rivers, intermittent streams. Woodland, scrubland, the infinite expanse of white sea.

She has lived her life by that map.

So much laid down by chance—

a bracelet of beads slipping off the wrist,

a smoldering pipe set down on a flat stone,

a mother and child lying down just there, under a bare-branched weeping willow, beside the creek too small to have a name, between Wounded

Knee and the Stronghold. After miles and miles of running, the woman can go no further. The snow sifts through the branches and gently covers them. She can see heaven closer than she ever thought it could be through the scrim of snow as she makes a cave of their two bodies.

3

Daniel holds Caro's head steady as she retches into the pan he keeps beside the bed. She has eaten so little that little comes up, just a thin stream of green bile that is agony, he knows, on her ulcerated tongue.

"Finished?" he asks, and strokes her scalp. She spits into the pan, nods, and falls back on the pillow.

"I think it's time for some Zofran." He consults the day's index card, an orderly schedule of drugs, doses, and times, which he files in a small plastic box on the nightstand.

She looks up at him with vacant eyes. "I... don't...know if—"

"I don't think you're in danger of overdosing on nausea meds, sweetheart."

He roots through the clutter on the nightstand—a dozen different supplements and appetite stimulants to counteract the anorexia, corticosteroid cream to control itching, plain old petroleum jelly for flaking lips. Next to the Vaseline is an unopened box of immediate-relief morphine auto-injectors for breakthrough pain, and a handful of empty syringes he had used to inject the Neupogen that bolstered Caro's white blood cell count during chemotherapy. And finally, there is the pharmacopoeia of prescription drugs, a rainbow of pills—bright red Docusate for the unremitting constipation, the forest-green wheels of Haldol for hallucinations, tiny white Versed for agitation. The Zofran is missing.

"I don't know how much...I can...," she says, "if I can—"

"Sure you can. They're the pills you take without water. No water, no throwing up. That's the theory, anyway."

"That's not...what I meant." She taps her forehead with her fist. "I meant...how much... how much..."

"Hold on," he says, and checks each pill bottle again while she continues to mutter to herself. He is usually so careful with her meds, especially the Zofran. At $22 a dose, its cost is nothing compared to the $300 vials of Neupogen—but still. A fair price, he supposes, for the reward: eliminating the nausea that before the drug's invention made chemotherapy and the cocktail of medications required for cancer treatment even more intolerable. Two years ago, after her first chemotherapy, he had gone to the pharmacy late on a Friday afternoon to fill the Zofran prescription. The insurance company refused to cover it without additional paperwork that would take until the following Monday to obtain. By that time, Caro would have spent the weekend poised over the toilet. The apologetic pharmacist, Mr. Canfield (whom Daniel had come to know in the past two years as Ralph, Ralph with his three kids and aging golden Labrador and the wife who used Zoloft) took pity on him, counted out eight tablets wrapped in individual silver blister packs, and slipped them into a Ziploc bag.

"This should outlast the nausea," he told Daniel. "But you need to hound the insurance company. Today. Ask for the supervisor, and the supervisor's supervisor. It's a matter of persistence," he said, "this whole ordeal. *Persistence*," he repeated, tapping one of the silvery domes housing the Zofran, as if that single word held the key to beating breast cancer.

Why persist? So that Caro could become part of a statistic? Not a wife, not a mother, just a percentage added to a percentage exceeding even the medical establishment's most optimistic projections of its vaunted goal to extend—

"—how much longer I can ... can ... "

She strains to form a simple sentence, and he thinks of her reading Milton for pleasure not all that long ago. "How much longer what, Caro?"

She looks at him, puzzled. "What?"

"Nothing."

"Oh." She gazes out the large picture window that frames the front lawn, staring at what he can only imagine, since the view has been obliterated by the night.

He turns away from her and crosses the bedroom to search her dresser for the missing medicine bottle. The usual disarray of its surface—hair clips and safety pins and odd receipts, a clutch of necklaces tangled on the mirrored vanity tray, a silk scarf tossed on the slip chair next to her dresser—all of it is missing. Now there are only objects arranged like curiosities on a museum shelf. A Styrofoam head holds her brown wig smoothed into a neat pageboy. Her mother's old vanity set, a sterling silver boar-bristle brush and hand mirror engraved with roses and leaves, lies flat and dusty beside the wig. And the carved rosewood and moonstone case he had bought for her in Shanghai hides jewelry she has not worn in months.

She had never really lived in this room. It was his office until she could no longer climb the stairs. A month ago, their son Henry and he transformed the study into the new master bedroom. A rented, queen-sized adjustable bed now filled the space that had been home to his prized Frank Gehry desk; their matching bureaus replaced two walls of teak bookshelves; and her pale gold slip chair—where she used to sit and smooth her stockings while they dressed for a night out—stood between her dresser and the picture window in the niche previously inhabited by his architect's drafting table.

"How much longer, how much longer?" Caro asks suddenly, close to tears. "What does that mean?"

He crosses back to the bed and hugs her. "Look, Caro, you've got to stop torturing yourself. You just lost your train of thought. It happens. It happens to everyone."

Her eyes are wide, her mouth slightly open, as if she wants to say something more. Instead she rests her head against his chest. He holds her for a minute, stroking her scalp until she relaxes in his arms.

"I'll be right back. I might've left the Zofran in the bathroom."

The medicine bottle lies open on the vanity sink where he does not remember leaving it. It's only 9:30, and already I'm losing it. How much longer, Caro dear? If that's a question, the answer is *too long.*

There is only one pill left, which means he will have to make yet another trip to the pharmacy to listen to Ralph's latest chapter on his dog's dementia or his wife's chronic depression. Perhaps he can prevail upon their daughter Alexandra to run the errand in the morning. Back in the bedroom, he offers Caro the Zofran tablet.

"No more," she says, pushing his hand away. "No more."

"You'll feel better if you take it."

He knows she knows he is lying. The medication

works only if she can keep it down long enough to take effect. Even without water, the pill nauseates her. Everything nauseates her. She has eaten so little in the past month, her face is bones and skin and not much else. *How can you change so completely?* He recalls this line from "'My Soul Is a Light Housekeeper,'" the poem she has made him read to her every day for the past week.

"Here you go," he says, pressing the pill into her palm. She hesitates; her look tells him she is calculating the effort it would take to change his mind. Her shoulders slump, and then she places the pill on her tongue and lets it dissolve.

"Satisfied?" She crosses her arms in front of her chest like a sulky child.

Say nothing, he tells himself. He counts to ten while she resettles on the pillow; the counting prevents him from telling her yet another lie. "Better?" he finally asks.

"A little." She grasps his left hand and squeezes it to hide her own lie.

He can tell she is struggling to keep the pill down. He traces the bones of her fingers to calm her, counting them, too, to pass the time. There are so many bones. He kisses her hand and says, "This is now bone of my bones."

"Flesh of my...flesh." She closes her eyes.

He listens to her breathing, shallow from the morphine, thready from the mucus she cannot fully clear from her throat.

"Audible respiration due to retained respiratory secretions," the doctor has warned him. One of the phrases in the peculiar language of impending death, this rasping that makes him feel as if *he* cannot breathe. He knows it will only worsen before she dies.

"How's the pain?" He touches the morphine pump clamped to an elastic band she wears around her waist.

"Manageable." Without opening her eyes, she pushes his hand away. "No more."

"Then sleep."

Her face relaxes as she settles into the bed, a rare moment of peace not shared by her body— a map of fresh bruises and fading scars. He has memorized every line, every blemish, so much so that he no longer sees what is right in front of him. The pale white incisions from the caesarean births of Alexandra and Henry. Needle marks and lesions from the hundred procedures she has endured in the past two years. The raised red gash where the port-a-catheter had been inserted to ease the administration of three failed chemotherapy regimens. That thing that grows from her navel. The missing breast.

You can get used to anything in time, he thinks. Not a vein in her body is inviolate by needles and knives, blood tests and intravenous morphine and forced hydration. This morning (was it just this morning?) Caro screamed as yet another vein was pierced when the hospice nurse changed the injection site for her morphine pump. The woman had numbed the skin with an anesthetic, but still the needle burned as it entered the vein. He scolded the nurse, who simply stared at him while she packed her black case and snapped it shut.

"How dare you reprimand her?" Caro said when they were alone. "It's *my* life!"

"But sweetheart—"

"My *life!*" she repeated, her face purple from the exertion of yelling. She looked to him then like an alien, her face distorted by tears and puffiness and patches of dry red skin, a body snatcher come to steal his beautiful, easy-going wife. Another line comes to him from the poem—*you're not the woman I thought I knew.* Is she?

She is. Resting now, her face has regained some of its pale beauty, and if he ignores the naked scalp and the blueblack circles under her eyes and the bony hollows of her cheeks, he can see in her the same grace that drew him to her twenty-five years before.

"Bone of my bones," he says again, but this time, she does not respond. Sleeping, he hopes, and with any luck, for the night.

4

In her dreams she lays three bones down in a limitless sea, three bones in a sea of white. What is their story? As if in reply, she is surrounded by books rising in columns reaching toward a solid pewter sky. She slides a leather journal from the stack nearest her. The column teeters slightly as the remaining books fall back into place, and then it continues to rise in concert with the other columns. In her mind a room is building, a room composed of books, books for walls stacked spine to spine, books for the floor laid end to end in endless planking. What were the heavens, gray and unremarkable, become a ceiling of books bearing down on her. She lifts the leather journal to cover her face, to ward off the inevitable deluge. Dust clogs her throat, she is suffocating in the airless space, there must be an exit. There is no exit. No windows, no doors, just walls, ceiling, floors. And then the movement ceases.

She peers out from behind the book she is holding. She will not drown, not yet, not in the books that surround her, or in her own breath.

The leather journal unfurls in her hands, the diary of a Frederick Hurst who passed through the Badlands bound for Montana to stake his claim on 160 acres of farmland. *In a fever,* the inky looping letters say, *the wagon rocking me to a final blessed sleep.* No, she thinks, the story is not in this dead white man's journal. She throws the book on the floor, runs her fingers along the spines of the tower closest to her, and finds a black hymnal embossed with the name Holy Cross Episcopal Church, red ribbons dangling from its gold-leafed edging. The songbook falls open. *O Lord my God,* it sings, *when I in awesome wonder, consider all the worlds Thy hands have made,* followed by a refrain of moans and sighs, and then the book flies out of her hands and melts into a far column. An Indian man's face looms before her, just his face, and he tells her, My wife is dead, and then fades away. A soldier in the corner salutes her, pivots ninety degrees, and melds with a wall of books. Mildewed pages, yellowed pages, pages so fragile they crumble in her hands, words so numerous they tumble together until they blend into a hum of voices speaking at once. Voices with stories to tell. So many voices, it is hard to hear only one, the mother's voice she is looking for. There is always one more voice, and one more beneath that:

Ee-nah, hay coo-e-yay... a song rises... on Wounded Knee Creek a great fire blazed... give up your guns and you will have food, they said... Black Coyote held onto his gun, and we told him, No... we observed the flag of truce, white flag wavering in the wind... a great storm was coming over the ridge... Yellow Bird believed in the Ghost Dance, believed the shirts would protect us... many who did not believe still wore the shirts... was that our sin?... Yellow Bird danced, threw a handful of dirt into the air... a soldier struggled with Black Coyote, struggled for his gun... a white man's voice—Fire! Fire on them!... what became of time?... bullets like rain, no, like knives... who was first?... everything equal, torn to pieces—bodies, clothing, plaited hair... the field enveloped in smoke... Big Foot's daughter ran toward her father... he was shot just before she reached him... her song... she gave a cry and stooped over him... her song rose... an officer seized a gun and shot her... her song rose over... and she fell across her father... her song rose over the valley... and she, too, died ... and her song mingled with the death songs of the warriors singing their deaths... *Ee-nah, hay coo-e-yay... Ee-nah, hay coo-e-yay... Misunkala cheyaya omaniye*, my little brother is crying for you...a sheet of fire...the brass buttons of the soldier's coat flew before me as he fell...we were flying, falling on all sides like grain before a scythe, the ground rocking and pitching like a canoe...I ran back to the tipi to find my wife...through the smoke I could see nothing but dead women and children...I thought I saw a black cloth masking a woman's face...but it was her braids shot off, hanging loose...a woman with an infant in her arms reached for the flag of truce...she was shot before she touched it...a child not knowing its mother was dead still nursed...a woman gone down to meet retreating survivors discovered her husband slaughtered... *Haŋ le miye što*...my son spoke bullets and then he died...women, little children came up the ravine and soldiers on both sides shot and shot until they killed every single one...the main firing lasted only ten minutes but what is that in time?...not thirty men and boys survived the first firings...scattered gunfire went on and on... the smell of blood wraps around me, sweet and nauseating...Mother carried my baby sister on her back, and she heard a shot behind her... children crying...horses running in every direction...a song...my father took my youngest brother down river, came crawling back empty-handed...a song rose... *Hunhun he, micinksi kte pelo*, your brother is dead...this song rose over the valley...white men thick like a pile of maggots and my little sister, her head blown off...Mother packed her in a papoose though she was dead...with cruel, deliberate aim the soldier shot a boy through both hips... four babies with crushed skulls...we found them in big heaps, women with children in their arms, young and old, horses and mules... sit up and be saved, the soldier said...one wounded man believed, raised up, and was shot dead by a soldier who did not hear the promise... *Ee-nah, hay coo-e-yay*, Mother, come back...why did He stand silently to let His people perish?

5

Tendrils of pain prick Daniel's right knee. Massaging it, he considers his options: an ice pack, ibuprofen he has lately been downing like M&Ms, good old-fashioned rest. Ice would require a trip to the kitchen, the ibuprofen is, no doubt, eating away his liver. Sleep, then, he thinks, though he knows his earlier nap, interrupted by Caro's wave of nausea, may have spoiled his chance for sleep. At least his knee will get the rest it deserves.

He lifts the covers, slides into the space warmed by Caro's body, and turns to face her. She is breathing shallowly but evenly, her earlier respiratory difficulties apparently eased. He licks the tips of his fingers and tames the errant hairs sticking up from her scalp. Ticking off the many ways in thought and in practice he has failed her today, he vows once again to be more patient, to listen more attentively, to respect her wishes. What it is like to be in her body, facing death, he cannot fathom. More than once, he has caught himself feeling relieved that he is not the one who is terminally ill. Sleep would cure him of this thinking, three days of precious, luscious sleep.

"Flesh of my flesh," he whispers into her ear, his voice blocking thoughts of how he has not measured up in the past two years to the man he believed he was. The grief therapist tells him these thoughts are normal, to be kind to himself, to forgive.

Last week he shouted at her, "How many spouses have *you* nursed through terminal illness?" The counselor sat there with her annoyingly sympathetic smile, nodding at his misplaced anger. She was all of thirty-five, plump, rosy-cheeked, with lustrous brown hair, and, as far as he knew, never married.

Be charitable, he thinks. Her marital status shouldn't matter.

Yet how can she even begin to understand the measure of his loss, the span from the first words of his marriage to the last? How could the simple vow, "I, Caroline, take you, Daniel, to be my husband," lead to mourners throwing dirt on his wife's coffin twenty-four years later?

No, that isn't right, he thinks. Surely the vow didn't lead to her illness.

And why in the night did he always return to this? He struggles to shake off thoughts of death, to turn his mind to something else, or to think of nothing, nothing but the yellow streetlight filtering through the branches of the sycamore just outside the room's picture window, throwing a deep red tracery of gnarled shadows against the terracotta walls. The colors of earth. He had chosen terracotta for his office, he told Caro, because its shading fluctuated so dramatically during the course of the day with the varying light from the windows that flanked three of the room's four walls: from the pale red created by the morning sun, to the deep sienna created by afternoon light, to the rich umbers of evening.

In the play of light and shadow above the dresser he notices the long filaments of an old cobweb draped from the wall to the ceiling directly over his head. Did Caro dust even up there? He sighs. Near the corner of the ceiling, a long-legged spider walks back and forth, tracing and retracing a single strand of silk that, in the low light of the bedroom, appears crystalline. This single thread is the anchor for a new web, and if he had the strength to reach up and squash the spider, he could eliminate the task of dusting the ceiling. What was the point? He imagined at that very moment a hundred spiders secreting themselves in every nook and cranny of his house, spinning their webs to prepare for a long night of trapping unsuspecting insects. Then, after a night's work, the spiders would consume the insects stuck in the sticky webs, leaving blasted threads dangling from corners and crevices. He had studied the architecture of wheel webs: sturdy, efficient, exposed.

The spider drops suddenly, swaying back and forth on a line of her own silk. Each movement increases her arc until she catches the original anchor thread at the corner. She drops again, swinging, swinging, and the silk thread glistens like wet glass, and he notices in the translucent silk a trace of blue, and then there is a blue light on a white bedspread somewhere in the past, the ribbon of blue light leading to a window. He follows the narrow path the light makes and finds at the end himself, twenty-four, undressing in the dark of a honeymoon suite lit only by the moon undulating on the Pacific waves. An apparition, this pear-shaped reflection of the moon moving up and down with each crest and shallow, and Caro's body, pure and wet, riding under his.

But something is wrong with this vision. They did not make love that night, their wedding night, but on a night seven days later. He knows he is asleep, he cannot move, but just the thought of the image from their real wedding night—of his wife unconscious and sprawled on the bathroom tile, her white nightgown twisted around her and her right breast spilling from the gown's lace edging—erases that of her beneath him a week later. He feels himself bending to wipe away the small streak of blood running down her forehead, then lifting her up and carrying her to bed.

—I think I'm going to throw up, she says, and she does, and he wraps her in the smooth white sheets, in the smooth white sheets and the vomit—

"I think I'm going to throw up."

It takes him a moment to realize that her words are not part of the lucid dream, a moment longer to shake off the paralysis of sleep so that he can help her. He grabs the metal pan and places it under her mouth and counts to himself, though the numbers refuse to form a pattern. Six, one, one, two, four, O, O, six, one, two. Then he understands: it is his telephone number.

"What do you think? Anything?"

"Nothing."

"That's good," he says. "Isn't it?"

She lies back in bed, not looking at him, not answering, and closes her eyes. He settles down beside her. The time he spent dozing felt like minutes, but already the spider has spun the spokes of her web and is halfway through connecting the spiral thread swirling from the center outward toward the bridge thread that forms the boundary of the web. Nimbly, she spans each width between the radii with her long legs. He concentrates on the spider, hoping to be lulled once again by the rhythmic motion of her web-making, but he suspects there will be no more sleep tonight.

The image of Caro wound in a white sheet comes back to him from the dream, and he shudders. He did not wind her in sheets that night, the first night of the long honeymoon spent in a suite scented with a dozen white roses and the brine of the sea. He had planned it all (he thought he could plan for everything) right down to her favorite roses.

White roses.

He had told her that she was his first. She, too, had wanted to wait, and so they waited until their wedding night, and then they waited six more days, through the gastroenteritis and the recovery, and on the seventh day they shared that night he had anticipated all his life. Over the years, he had told her more than once he was glad they waited.

Did she know then of the Mother's Day tradition in which men with living mothers wore red roses on their lapels and those whose mothers were dead wore white ones? Of course not. They had only become aware of the custom themselves when his own mother died ten years before. After church services the following Mother's Day, they bought white roses from the Women's Guild who sold them in the vestibule. How was it they had never noticed those white roses before? That year and every year since, Caro and he visited the cemetery where his mother was buried, knelt on the cool wet ground that covered her grave beside the empty rectangle of manicured lawn where his father would someday lie, and laid white roses on the bright green grass.

But perhaps Caro *had* known about white roses.

He runs his finger lightly along the raised, curved scar where her right breast had been, the ridge visible through her thin nightgown. She does not flinch; she must be sleeping soundly. The stitches left faint cross-hatchings on either side of the place where the surgeons cut two years ago. She had woken from the anesthetic, blind without her contacts. Better that she was blind. There were tubes everywhere, pumping fluids and draining fluids, Ringer's lactate and a catheter for urine, two drain bulbs filled with bloody fluid he would empty every day for a week, measuring their output and tracking the volumes on an index card, and praying his clumsiness did not hurt her more than she already hurt.

The scar under his finger is a hard ridge that has not softened with age as the surgeon had promised. Caro scarred easily and not well. It was one reason she had resisted the reconstructive surgery that would have restored the breast. Flap surgery to tunnel skin, fat, and muscle from her back to her chest wall, a second procedure to insert the saline implant, a third to fashion a new areola and nipple from the skin of her inner thigh, and to cut open her left breast in an upside-down T and lift it to match the right. The doctors had explained it all in gory detail.

"It wouldn't be my body," she told him. "I won't be the bride of Frankenstein."

"I'd still be your Mr. Frankenstein." His teasing

did not have the effect he had hoped for: her trademark eyeroll or a stifled groan or even the barest hint of a smile. Instead she had run to their bedroom, locked the door, and stayed there all afternoon. He knocked twice, but neither time did she answer.

They never spoke of the surgery again. Nevertheless she had tried to hide the scar from him, to deny the existence of the missing breast when she stepped from the shower almost three months after her mastectomy, her bald gray scalp glistening with the sheen of water, the skin under her eyes so transparent he could count the veins. He was shaving. He caught her reflection in the mirror: the scar where her breast had been was almost black from the heat of the water, a separate living thing throbbing with the pulse of her.

She saw that he saw her and pulled the towel over her missing breast. The mirror image of her left breast made it seem for a moment as if the right one had been miraculously restored. He closed his eyes, and then he opened them, turned away from the mirror and moved toward her, looking only at her face, looking all the while at her face, and then he kissed her on the mouth. He willed himself to kiss her. She was a beautiful woman once, the woman who had spun in the lamplight seven nights into their honeymoon, spun so fast it was as if the waves of white chiffon and lace could thrust her upward like blades of a propeller—

The slap of her body against the tile. The echo afterward. And Daniel stopped undressing in the darkened honeymoon suite.

She had fallen on the cold white tile, her nightgown twisted around the length of her body, her right breast exposed above the gown's lace border. He lifted her up and carried her to bed, nursed her for six days to the rush and crash of waves against rock.

He lifted her up and carried her to bed, her body still damp from the shower, her skin still warm from the steam. The heat of her, alive, under his tongue. He kissed her and did not stop kissing her, running his tongue over her shaved scalp where her long brown hair had been, the hair he buried his face in the first time he came inside her, the silken dampness of her hair against his face a memory that returned and returned. He ran his tongue over her bare scalp and down her neck, slipped his fingers under the towel, and pulled it away. She was shaking. Like the first time they made love, only then it was because the desire was so powerful that she started shaking even before he touched her. She had danced in the lamplight, spinning above the earth, and when she came down, gently this time, not fainting, not falling, he had taken her to bed. He almost forgets those first awkward moments, their teeth clacking and the clumsy explorations of fingers and tongues and trying to find her and they both laughed and he said, How hard can this be? Teenagers figure this out, and she said, It's not hard, not hard at all, and she guided him inside her and she was right.

It wasn't hard, he told himself when he first kissed the scar where her breast had been. He kissed her scar and with every kiss the scar became just another part of her, something new in the fabric of her skin, a long dark seam brilliant against the white. She was alive, yes, alive, and every minute he kissed her, he fought the urge not to kiss her, counting each tiny ghost of a cross-stitch, a dozen kisses to cover every inch of the scar that was, after all, only another part of her. And then the rest of the body, her body and his, rediscovering that first rhythm, the same rhythm they had recaptured on so many lost nights guided by the memory of other lost nights under the dark dark cover of darkness. She had hidden her body from him as she aged. All those years he should have told her what he thought of covering, the dark room, the feel of his tongue against her scalp, against the long line of her clavicle, the comfort of his face buried in her hair on a thousand unremembered nights.

How can she hide now? So much of her body has been exposed by illness—her scalp, her veins, her bones. Even the tumor on her navel looks as if it is trying to escape, as if her body is turning itself inside out. Soon every part of her will be visible to him. She might as well be made of glass, smooth and clear as glass, and he leans into her, runs his nose along her neck. She is warm, still warm, and the taut cord of her neck still pulses with blood.

"Dietrich," she says.

"What?" he says. "It's me. Daniel."

She mouths something that sounds like "hand me."

"You need something?" He searches the nightstand for anything that might do.

She grabs his hand, though her eyes remain closed. "Tell me what you have come to tell me."

"What do you want, Caro?"

She whispers one thing clearly, "'Language bears the burden of the sacred.'" Then she is quiet.

He rolls away from her and stares at the ceiling. The spider has disappeared, though the finished web wafts on currents of air. He finally spies her, curled motionless in a brown ball in the center of the web, waiting or sleeping or perhaps even dead. How would he know?

6

She sleeps with Dietrich in the tent of bones, in the excavated pit of bones. She sleeps with him in the garbage, Sioux garbage. Under the weight of their bodies rising and falling, the bones shift, carelessly reorganized in the trench whose meticulously tagged geological layers mark the passage of long periods of time.

Her breath catches in her throat.

—Are you all right? he asks.

—It hurts. My back.

In an instant he is underneath her, and she has risen above him. She looks down at him then, in the scant light making its way through the smudge of the plastic tent window. Sweat-shined, expectant, his face is a map of thirty years spent in deserts like this, the limitless map of the vanished. He is the twenty-two-year-old woman making love for the first time. He is Dietrich who has lost count of the virgins.

—Have you ever been in love? she asks him later, when her breathing has returned to normal.

—Dear girl, he says, and gently cups her right breast, *this* is love. Then he pinches her nipple until she cries out. —And so is that.

§

She falls into a deeper sleep. Daniel strokes himself until he comes.

§

She drifts up to consciousness, the scent of salt air surrounding her. The sea in their room and the Pacific outside and the great white unbroken sea of Kansas and the Dakotas. Dietrich lies beside her in the bed.

—Did you know that sea serpents can live their entire lives in water? he says, tracing the snake-like scar on her chest. —Imagine their surprise when this great sea dried into the white dust before us. That's how we find them, their mouths open in surprise.

She turns away from Dietrich to find Daniel, the scent of the sea even stronger with him. Far away, a breeze streams through an open window, and within the wind the rush of the ocean rises through her dream. In the mirror is a woman not herself. The stranger is pulling silver hairpins from an elaborate French twist, lining their pearl tips two by two on the bathroom's marble sink. She is an Ark sailing across a white sea, moving slowly as if in a dream. It is a dream.

—Mrs. Daniel Singleman, she says to the woman for the first time.

The name feels like a winter coat tried on in summer. It is summer, a moonlit night. Through the wall she can see a dozen white roses fan out on a white bedspread. A bar of light flows from her to Daniel and merges into a continuous stream beyond the cliff. Naked, he presses his fingertips to the bedroom window, touches the shimmering light on the dark waves. The waves heave, and she is sick, briefly, in the toilet.

In her hands is her mother's bridal shower gift, a white chiffon nightgown. No time for dilly-dallying. How to pretend? It's an old trick, after all. She pulls the nightgown over her head, fingers the folds in the sheer fabric, smoothes the beaded lace edging. At her bridal shower she had a fleeting vision of her wedding night: this wedding night, that dream. She lifts the toilet lid and bends over, feeling momentarily like she is going to be sick. The food at the reception was too rich, the icing too sweet, though she hardly ate anything. And then there was her mother, pressing condoms into her hand. Was this Mom's idea of a heart-to-heart? A cold washcloth on her forehead, and the nausea passes.

—Caro, is that better?

She has fallen, the smooth, hard tile against her cheek. It is Daniel who has put the damp washcloth on her forehead, who lifts her up, who settles her on the cool sheets. Breath on her neck, a hand on her thigh, the weight of a man's body on hers. She feels pain, kisses his shoulder, sinks her teeth there. She is sick. The food at the reception too rich, the icing too sweet, she is sick in the toilet. The damp washcloth on her forehead. And then there were her mother's lips pressed to her cheek. Good-bye. Good-bye.

Whose hips bear down on hers? Who hovers above her, caressing her face? —You're hurting me, she says.

The cleansing scent of salt air turns into the odor of wasting fish and splayed mollusks putrefying in the sun, and the sea dries up and all that is left is chalk and bones, layers of bones, titanothere and sea serpent, mother and son, Dietrich and she, the bones under them.

—Who's there?

It is Dietrich, kissing her breast tenderly where he has hurt her. The next day the nipple is a darkish purple stain in a sea of honey, a stain that never goes away. No, it is only her mother talking to her. It is only her mother. It must be a dream, her mother dead and buried far away. His tongue slow on her now is all the soothing she needs.

—Dear girl, what would it be like to live an entire life underwater, with nothing but the sea, and this occasional taste of salt?

7

Did her husband die quickly in the storm of bullets?

Did her widowed mother suffer?

Did the ghost dancers leave their footprints in the earth surrounding the tree of peace?

Did she cup her son's body to her own as she ran north along the ice-choked creek toward the Stronghold?

Did the creek offer her its comforts: its familiar rills, its turns and tuck-ins, the lullaby of current swirling through sheets of ice?

Did she stop along the bank to pray? —*Grandfather, Great Spirit, have pity on me, a pitiful girl with a child in her arms. The faces of the dead surround me, and I am afraid.*

Did her husband die with honor?

Did they know her widowed mother's body by the mutilated pinky?

Did she leave her footprints in the soft mudbank as she ran along the nameless creek?

Did she think the Stronghold meant safety?

Did she find comfort in remembering the day Little Magpie, his face painted red, stole upon a nest of yellow-jackets and, with a rush and war whoop, vanquished the killers?

Did she console herself with words? —*Grandfather, Great Spirit, I have no one to pray to but you. Give me courage so that I may use the dead to guide me.*

Did she dream of her husband buried in the earth, in a grave beside her mother, in the sacred land where her father had lain for so many years, to give her strength to run on and on?

Did she notice the snow starting to fall?

Did she search then for the eddy under the weeping willow where she used to play her games as a girl?

Did she remember her son's own games of mud and willow, his sledding down a winter hill on a sheet of bass-wood bark?

Did she recall his tears when the yellow-jackets stung him?

Did one day of her pain compare to another, pulling stingers from her son's feet with bone tweezers to pulling bullets from his braids with her bare hands?

Did she pray? —*Grandfather, Great Spirit, hear me. My son is dead. Help me face the wind and the snow and walk the right road to my own death.*

8

"I'm thirsty," Caro says in her sleep. Moths alight on her mouth, they drink, and she knows that is why she is always thirsty.

§

Is she dreaming, Daniel wonders, or does she need something to drink? He rubs an ice chip along her flaking lips, and she opens her mouth and takes it with her tongue. The tip of her tongue caressing his fingers causes in him an involuntary spasm of desire.

Her eyes flutter open. "The moths are thirsty," she says in a ragged whisper.

Where is she? He raises her to a sitting position, brings the water glass to her lips, and inserts the straw in her mouth. The liquid bubbles weakly up the clear plastic cylinder until all that is left is the static of water draining from the glass.

He places the empty glass on the nightstand. The hollow thunk against the wooden surface reminds him that the house has been unnaturally quiet. It is close to midnight, and he wonders if the kids went to bed without saying goodnight. That would be unusual, but they would also know better than to disturb their parents if they had found them asleep earlier in the evening.

"That's strange," he mutters, smoothing the blanket and tucking it under her chin. "I haven't heard the kids all night."

She burrows her head into the pillow but says nothing.

"Maybe I should go check on them? What do you think?" He touches her shoulder. "Caro?"

One of the blessings of morphine: she has fallen instantly asleep. He rises from the bed and turns to leave, starting when she suddenly tugs his arm.

"Go on," she says, "kiss them goodnight for me."

He lingers as her eyes close and her face relaxes into its customary lines and creases: the soft folds of her eyes, mouth, and chin: the comfort of the familiar. She is, in many ways, in the essential ways, the same woman he met during his final semester at Haverford College. He was writing the thesis required of all Cities majors, which he would have to defend like a master's thesis the following month. He had chosen Growth and Structure of

Cities, the fancy name for a major available only at Haverford's sister college, Bryn Mawr, for the basest of reasons: he thought it would force him to talk to women. Skulking across the campus like a cipher, he had barely opened his mouth in four years except to answer questions in class that he was sure he knew. At night he would retreat to his single room at Haverford; sometimes whole days passed without his talking to anyone.

When he spied Caro that March night, she was sitting in a carrel in the unbroken silence of Bryn Mawr's Canaday Library basement, sipping a can of Tab and chewing on a pink rubber eraser, and poring over an ancient text on archaeology. Two floors below ground, the space was illuminated only by the artificial light of sizzling overhead fluorescents, a warren of shelving crammed floor to ceiling with rarely used books and even more rarely used carrels.

He had noticed her on campus before; he had watched her for four years from a distance. She was hard to miss—at five-feet-ten, she towered over most of the other women and carried that height with the grace of a dancer. She was a trained dancer, he later discovered, and though by her own admission she would never have made prima ballerina, the essence of the grace learned from the studied movement of ballet had stayed with her, lodged like memory in her muscles and bones. It was the way she moved that first attracted him— gliding across campus as if her feet barely needed the earth, a skinny, multicolored scarf trailing behind her even on the warm days of spring. She was, for him, unattainable. He lacked the ability for even the simplest opening line—where are you from? what dorm do you live in? would you... would you... and then he morphed into a stuttering imbecile. No, he would never do more than watch her glide across campus.

He had spent so much of his senior year alone among the subterranean stacks working on his thesis that he almost forgot he had a voice. The library was a comfort in that way—you were not required to talk. In fact, the rules forbade it. He found his companionship in old books so infrequently checked out it was as if the authors had written them especially for him, private epistles sent across the ages. His senior thesis concerned the German architect Bruno Taut, whose utopian vision of monumental crystalline buildings arrayed in the sunlight across the Alps captured his imagination. He had chanced upon Taut's *Alpine Architektur* the previous year, and that slender book led to Taut's Crystal Chain correspondence with other leading German modernist architects of the 1920s. Taut wanted no less from his glass architecture than to fuse art and social reform, to transform the closed culture of his country after the Great War by exposing its society to the possibilities of social integration through architecture.

Daniel was captivated by the practical challenges of Taut's vision—the innovations in glass manufacture all-glass buildings would require, and the methods of hiding a building's infrastructure so that the illusion of continuous expanses of glass could be maintained. Where to put the pipes? the wiring? the ventilation? And if one could overcome these challenges, if buildings could be composed entirely of glass, why not whole cities? Then there were the sociological implications. How would opening rooms to light, letting in the colors and textures of the natural world, affect human perception of the environment? How would transparency, re-envisioning the world in Taut's spirit of empathy, prove his claim that architecture could alter for the better the way people lived?

Daniel had looked for the answers in the pages of these old books. That March night, while Caro chewed her eraser into damp crumbs and sipped her illicit can of Tab, he paced the aisle behind her, pretending to read a text on Gropius's screen wall system—designed to allow external glass walls to continue without interruption—as he watched her body appear and disappear between clusters of racked books. What was a girl like her doing down in the basement? He reached for another book, and it was only then he noticed his hands were shaking. He admonished himself. Even in this closed space, and even if she looked his way, he did not have to talk to her. He could simply nod and bury his nose in a book. And yet he could not stop his hands from shaking.

How was it he attracted Caro in the first place? Was it the shock of rare books sliding one by one to the floor, their dull thuds echoing in the empty aisles? Was it finding him covered in the books that he, in an attempt to stop their tumbling, instead set off in a further avalanche by tripping and falling against the shelves?

She is there, the campus goddess, taller than he imagined and so young, so very young, her hair swept up in a sloppy pony tail with a bright yellow pencil sticking out of it and just a single line of worry wrinkling her smooth forehead.

"Are you all right?" she asked, extending her hand to him. He was too stunned to take it.

He said, "Uh," a noise like choking, or hocking phlegm, and then "uh" again. He swallowed. "It's just that these books... the books... there are so many books." Yes, a stuttering imbecile.

"I thought I was the only weirdo who stalked the B-level." She stuck both arms straight out in front of her and rolled her eyes so far back in her head that all he could see were the whites. Stiff-legged, cheeks sucked in, she mimicked a perfect zombie from *Night of the Living Dead*, tottering back and forth in front of him.

He found his voice beneath the phlegm. "How do you do that, the eye thing?"

"Sworn to secrecy," she said, and crossed her heart with her fist. "Now look what a mess you've made!" Then somehow she was sitting beside him, talking to him as if she had known him for years. While they sorted through the Dewey Decimal coding, she told him about osteology and the carbon-dating of bones, the search for the first Americans, and her plans to participate in a year-long archaeological dig in the Badlands of South Dakota. He told her of his cities of glass, of his belief that the very way people interacted with their neighbors could be changed through architecture.

"But to make it practical," he said, "that's the challenge."

"Practical? Why would you want to expose yourself to such scrutiny? Would nothing be hidden? To design glass buildings as expressions of social equality while keeping our private lives private—isn't that the bigger challenge?"

"That's it exactly. To balance the public and private," he said, as if he had only just thought of the theory's implications, "you can work with the properties of glass. It's transparent, but it can also distort. It lets light pass through, but it can also reflect and refract that same light. A single wall of glass might only blur the boundary between inside and outside. Multiple walls, one behind the other, can bend light in interesting ways and create the illusion of depth."

Caro did not yawn or roll her eyes, as some of his classmates had done. Encouraged, he went on to describe how these properties could be used to foster a sense of solitude and privacy as well as communion with nature and empathy with others. As he spoke, he drew Taut's *Der Felsendom*, the *Cathedral in the Rocks*, its glass columns and arches and domes nestled in the crook of a stony canyon. She bent closer, tracing one of the central spires. He sketched the even more ambitious *Tal mit Wasserstürzen*, the *Valley with Cascades*, and in its interplay of terraced glass structures and tumbling waterfalls, he recreated Taut's imaginary Alpine realm under open sky and rainbow. It was, he thought, the most beautiful of the German's visions.

"Could this be done?" Caro asked. "Could you actually build something like this?"

"I think so. That's what I'm working on. But this kind of architecture would require change. And change," he said, quoting the last line of his thesis with a theatrical bow, "is the triumph of humanity over politics."

She laughed at him. "Really? Can politics ever be humane? Just look at what happened to Taut's fellow Germans after World War I. Change is usually brought about by catastrophe, one catastrophe after another—war, famine, plague."

"But it *can* be otherwise."

We *were* young, he thinks. Change was right, yes, change was right, and that rightness would remain immutable in the face of other changes. We could stop time. We could build cities of glass, make rooms to house the sun and the stars, the trees and the mountains. Why not?

One of his fellow Cities majors—a Melanie Jane Something-Something—had written her thesis on wind power, the logical energy source of the future. Clean, cheap, abundant. She envisioned windmills whirling on America's empty prairies and gust-battered seacoasts, wind farms designed by Louis Kahn and I. M. Pei and Alexander Calder. Why not form and function?

Naïveté, he laughs to himself. That's what we suffered from. It wasn't terminal.

Caro's strained inhalation breaks his reverie. At least Melanie Jane was out there somewhere, still nursing her wounded dreams, still able to breathe without the continuous drip-drip-drip of morphine. Or she could be dead. For all he knew, no one was spared.

He lifts Caro's head and slides another pillow underneath, then bends his ear to her mouth. Listening intently, he cannot tell if she is simply breathing more easily or if she is breathing at all.

"Why are you still here?" she whispers in his ear. "Did something happen to the kids?

"The kids!" he says, hitting his forehead with his open palm. He had almost forgotten the children. "Sorry, I was too busy watching you."

"Right," she says, and touches her scalp. "Your goddess."

"You read my mind."

"Liar."

He kisses the top of her head. "Sleep."

9

If hearing is the last sense to leave the body, then snowfall whispering over their faces, over itself, is the last thing they hear. Blankets laid gently one on top of another, nothing else. No weeping, no iron nail driven into pine board, no lamentation but snow sweeping over them, whispering its final prayer: *Come, Grandmother, Great Spirit, hold them gently in your arms.* Caro hears this whispering, soft, softer now, and finally the quiet rustling of sheets.

There is beauty in the white sea, a mother and her small son, petrified in a posture of love, his blood on her, her life in him, both listening to the snow whisper, Come.

Their bodies are flesh, flesh and bone. The flesh blackens along the skin's surface where gravity presses it to earth—along hip and leg and foot, along the soft pad of the mother's right arm and the hand that yet grips the spent bullet from the boy's braid—as the fluids freeze close to the layer of skin that touches the frozen ground. The bones are wood, staves of a hull. The mother's face no longer resembles the face the boy loved; his face no longer her beloved. Yet the two still cling to each other, the woman cupped around the boy, the boy's hands grasping her forearms. Cold, bittersweet in its protections, preserves them through the long Dakota winter.

And then the animals, the masked shrew and the free-tailed bat, the pocket gopher and the prairie vole, the yellow-bellied marmot and the black-footed ferret, the grasshopper mouse and the flying squirrel, the mink and the badger, the black bear and the white-tailed jackrabbit, the bison and the pronghorn, the gray wolf and the red fox, emerge from their winter dens. The coyotes, too, emerge, coyotes who long ago marked this land for their own.

In the rocky outcropping that serves as shelter, a mother coyote labors to give birth. She is panting; perspiration coats her black muzzle, her fur is matted to her flanks. Her mate prowls back and forth in front of the entrance. A female stays within to help with the birth, makes a nest of grass and fur on which the mother lies down to begin the active part of labor. Soon four pups, a male and three females, blind, limp-eared, pug-nosed, lie bloodied on the bedding. One fledgling pup, the second born—a little boy, the only boy—roots in the underside of his mother's body, finds purchase, and begins to suckle.

10

Plunged into the sudden darkness of the unlit hallway, Daniel waits for his eyes to adjust. The children *must* be upstairs sleeping, he reassures himself. Not a single speck of light leaks into the surrounding pitch. Caro and her suffering behind him, and nothing but a thick wall of nothing in front. It could be his familiar hall, with family photographs lining the walls and the long oriental runner cushioning his steps, or it could be a wormhole, a one-way tornado to Oz, the rabbit-hole to Wonderland.

And how *did* you feel when you realized you'd left your old life behind, Mr. Singleman? Toto, we're not in Kansas anymore. Would you tell me, please, which way I ought to go from here? Things were getting curiouser and curiouser. Good-bye, feet! Man Leaves Bedroom in Time for Hatter's Tea-Party.

—Why is this life like any other life?

—I give up. What's the answer?

—I haven't the slightest idea.

—I think you might do something better with Time than to waste it with riddles that have no answers.

—If you knew Time as well as I do—

(Am I losing my mind?)

—you wouldn't talk about wasting *it*! It's *him*—

(I *am* losing my mind.)

—I dare say you never even spoke to Time.

Daniel closes his eyes, and then opens them. The hallway is black. No Mad Hatter, no Tea-Party. He knows those words by heart because Alexandra had forced him years ago to read *Alice in Wonderland* over and over again, his daughter mistaking for the longest time Lewis Carroll's book as her own: *Alex in Wonderland*.

But wouldn't a fate of speaking in riddles be better than this, even if the Hatter and the Dormouse and the March Hare played musical chairs and bickered endlessly? Does God exist? Why do we suffer? And why *is* a raven like a writing desk? On second thought, I'd simply fall into a whole new set of worries. In that other life, the books would never have fallen, and I'd never have met Caro, and I'd not have the children. And then?

Consoled by the very emptiness of the space in front of him, he waits for his pupils to expand, for his eyes to gradually discern shape and shadow, the hard edges of the hall table, the squat outline of the lowest stair, the flaming red exit sign.

When the fluorescent lights on B-level suddenly shut off at three that morning, Caro and he discovered that the library had closed around them. They whispered in the darkness until they could see well enough to make their way to the elevator. The security guard, who had fallen asleep at his desk by the front entrance, made them empty their backpacks and turn their pockets inside out. He pawed through their belongings and confiscated the unchecked library book Caro had accidentally stuffed in her backpack along with the lone remaining Tab.

The guard shook the soda can in her face and threatened to have their library privileges revoked. "I can do it, you know," he said. "I have the power."

Instead of being chastened, they began to giggle, and Caro, choosing that moment to cross her eyes behind the guard's back, only made things worse. Suddenly the whole world seemed comical, the security guard with his silver badge and imitation leather policeman's hat, Taylor Hall with its mock-Gothic appointments, even the trees of Senior Row casting eerie pre-dawn shadows. Something had overtaken him that otherworldly morning, something he did not fully understand. When the guard patted him down like a criminal, Daniel offered to take off his clothes as well. He performed a mock strip tease, and all the while Caro and he, under the influence of too much caffeine and too little sleep, could not stop laughing. What had come over him to flout the rules so boldly? The guard escorted them outside, still threatening their library privileges, and loudly turned the keys in the lock as they held on to each other to keep from falling.

A small seam of light emerges from the opposite end of the hallway. The light startles him, and then he realizes everything is quiet, too quiet. His heart registers the familiar rhythm of panic. The kids are upstairs sleeping, that's all, he tells himself as he mounts the steps two by two.

A lamp has been left on inside the curio cabinet in the upstairs hall, but otherwise everything is dark. He steadies himself against the cabinet, one hand on its smooth wood frame and the other on his chest. His heart is working furiously against its natural rhythm, and he wonders if this is the beginning of a heart attack. Since when has climbing the stairs left him winded? But the children, he thinks.

"Easy," he whispers, "easy." It would not do to burst into the kids' rooms at midnight, with their mother downstairs dying and their father frantically gasping for air. He looks toward their bedrooms, dark as tar, quiet as an empty church, exactly as they should be this late at night.

"See," he says aloud. "They're fine."

His heart returns to its simple one-two, one-two, one-two. He presses his forehead to the cool glass front of the cabinet door, breathing steadily as the pressure in his chest subsides. Behind the glass are the family's Buried Treasures, so named by Alex many years ago. There are marbles and coins, rocks and shells and smooth stones, sand and leaves and dried flowers. Always the professional archaeologist, Caro had labeled each specimen in square black letters. In two baby food jars, one each for Alex and Henry, Caro had collected her children's lost baby teeth. Next to them, on a flat piece of shale, she had written "Lascaux 1985," the year before Alex was born, the year of their visit to the Dordogne caves and the paintings of the hemiones and the aurochs and the unicorn. Beside the shale is a perfectly shaped, chambered nautilus Alex had found at the Jersey shore when she was eight, "Cape May 1994" stenciled in black on the underside. An iridescent swirl of blue shot through with gold had drawn her to the shell, the gold glinting in the summer sun when she raised it to Daniel's ear and said, It's a whole other world talking at once, Daddy, and he nodded yes as if he believed a city of tiny beings dwelled within that shell, within each chambered vesicle, the wind's echo so much like a polyphony of voices, and grains of sand so white sparkling on his daughter's pink cheek, and it could be, it could very well be, another world in that vortex. What did he know? And what had become of his fairy-tale Alex now so consumed with becoming real, a daughter soon to be motherless? Don't think that way, don't think it, but a small jar filled with black-flecked sand beckons, the sand from what had become, he suddenly realizes, the final family vacation. The trip to Puerto Rico the Christmas before last was a celebration: Caro was in remission. She wore bright scarves to protect her bald head and oversized sunglasses to shield her eyes because chemo had left her more sensitive to the sun. She was beautiful that week, a slight, so slight blush returned to her skin and her high-pitched laughter and her pulling him close to sneak a sudden kiss as they walked hand-in-hand on the beach. Jackie O, he called her, and Henry said, Who?, and Caro laughed and said, Jacqueline Kennedy, of course, and Henry said, Oh, yeah, the lady in the pink suit, and then she kissed him too. Would a stranger have guessed that she was dying?

The last relic on the shelf is a small piece of amber from the Badlands, which glows in a gold halo created by the cabinet's museum lamp. An odd discovery, Daniel thinks, on an archaeological dig where Caro had unearthed mostly discarded animal bones. He opens the cabinet door, picks up the stone, and holds it up to the light. Its surface is smooth, almost oily. A scattering of dark freckles clouds the stone's core—specks of dirt, or tiny splinters of rock, or maybe even a flicker of prehistoric life. Curious, he peers through the semitransparent stone, but there is no way to tell with certainty what is captured in this strange souvenir from South Dakota.

They had three months together before Caro left for the Badlands. The night before she left, he proposed with a ring his mother bestowed for the occasion, a simple gold band with a quarter-carat diamond. "I know this seems fast," he said to her, clearing his throat, clearing it again. "I know...but would you...you know?" he asked, and she said, "Yes," and he slipped the ring on her finger before she changed her mind, or realized what question she was answering.

At the airport, he met the dig's supervisor, Professor Something or Other, who expounded to those acolytes gathered around him how they were going to trace the "limitless map of history." Bullshit, he thinks now, he thought then. His dislike for the man extended not only to his arrogance, but to the fact that he had won a grant that allowed him to pursue his life's dream. That, and he was a man, and Caro was the only woman on the team.

"You're imagining things! He's ancient—at least as old as my father. And besides," she whispered in his ear, "there's hair growing out of his nose."

They kissed one last time as her plane was boarding, and she turned at the mouth of the jetway and waved. He returned the gesture, feeling finally like an adult, his fiancée off to South Dakota to find the first Americans and he to Yale to become an architect. Yet there was something in the way she spoke to him on the phone that night and the nights that followed, something he could not quite place, the space between them already greater than the thousands of miles separating them. He could only imagine her (which he often did) kneeling in the dust and bones and hardscrabble earth—streaks of dirt smeared across the definitive line of her jaw, her hair pulled back in a high, severe pony tail that accentuated the delicate structure of her face and the slight concavity of her temples—patiently scraping away each layer of earth, discovering in those early weeks of the dig only evidence of the casual inhabitation of the Sioux.

The discouragement in her voice heartened him. Soon she would realize that recovering evidence of the first humans in prehistoric America was something akin to winning the lottery, only more difficult. The prevailing theory was that the first Americans arrived in the New World 11,500 years ago over a land bridge called Beringia that linked Siberia and Alaska. The culture was named Clovis after a distinctive, fluted stone spear point archaeologists unearthed near Clovis, New Mexico, in 1937, a point later found scattered widely throughout the United States and less widely to the south. But Caro's Professor Whoever was convinced there was something even older in South Dakota.

"The man's obsessed. A complete lunatic," she told him on the phone one night not long before they suspended the dig for the winter. "Screams at us for not working hard enough while we squat in the dirt with our fingers bleeding. He knows it might take years, assuming there's anything down there." Then she sighed and ticked off the day's finds. "Bison bones and a fire pit and more bison bones. I thought last week I'd found a tiny human finger bone. But the professor said it was only a shard from a clay pipe. Sioux garbage."

He listened to her chronicle of ordinary human existence and reassured her that every day she dug was one day closer to whatever she was looking for, but secretly he hoped that she would give up. Who was he to have wished failure on her so young?

Days later, she uncovered the rounded cup of a woman's pelvis cradling a small piece of skull. On the phone that night, she had trouble forming sentences, and because language was her first love, he worried that she was ill.

"Two human bone fragments," she said. "A woman's pelvis and a piece of frontal bone." Then in a rush, "And that pipe I found? Remember? The tiny bit of pipe? A thumb bone, Daniel. The professor mistook it for pipe. Pipe," she said. "Can you believe it?"

During the winter hiatus, the team catalogued the finds, analyzed and conserved bones, carbon-dated select remains. She identified the skull and thumb bones as those of a child, the pelvis as that of a young woman who had been through childbirth. In those bones, she told him, she saw a vision, a Miniconjou Sioux mother and child dying together in a snowstorm after Wounded Knee.

Alone in his shabby New Haven apartment, with Caro existing as only a disembodied voice, he could sense the power of those three bones. He pressed the receiver to his ear, bringing her as close to him as possible, and though he possessed her in that moment, and though they planned a summer wedding, he could see her drifting away on the unbroken white sea of which she spoke so incessantly, as if the canvas tent that sheltered her were a sail and the earth a raft and together they carried her farther and farther into the past. This was a recurring dream of his, Caro drifting away with her professor on a boat made of canvas and earth.

Does every man think his wife attractive enough to be the envy of other men, or was it merely his own vain shortcoming? It strikes him now that at some point he had stopped worrying that other men might find her desirable. When had his fear subsided? After Alex? After Henry? After chemo?

In her long absence, he was not idle. He studied architecture and its impact on the form of the city, how changes in design might affect the psychology of those who inhabited the darker landscapes of urban America. He sketched skyscrapers impossible to build: towers of glass that would maximize light filtering down to the concrete and macadam of the street level, green spaces that would let the natural world into urban dwellings, beauty in previously unimaginable places. Yale's program required him to submit a design for the Vietnam Veterans Memorial competition. His proposal evoked Taut's Utopia of shimmering glass monuments staggered across the Alps, only Daniel's monuments were nameless tombstones in an empty expanse of grass. He lost himself in cities for the living and the dead, cities composed of glass and light, forgetting in his absence from himself that Caro would not return, that he had only theory to offer her against the tangible, the discovery of a world once a single place unbroken by time, of the Badlands and Pangaea, of what she called Eden. He heard this distance in her voice widen when, in the spring, the team unearthed the first clues of a mammoth kill site, and worse, a bone tool that pre-dated Clovis, an artifact at least 15,000 years old. The invisible line connecting them grew fainter. Her leaving him became something he feared and expected, a terminal destination at the end of twelve months' travail.

And then she was calling from her parents' house in upstate New York.

"The Sioux are right," she told him that night, "the dead should never be disturbed."

That was all she said about South Dakota at the time. Relieved that she had returned, he did not press her for details about why she had come home a month early.

He touches the radiant piece of amber in his palm, all that was left of those months of uncertainty and loneliness. They seem inconsequential now, as slight as the smooth stone in his hand. Yet in the incandescent light he can, if he looks hard enough, imagine an insect caught in a slow slide of molten rock and preserved against the intrusions of man for all eternity. He kisses the stone and slips it into his pocket before entering Alex's bedroom.

11

Snow dances down the ridge, small maelstroms twisting above the earth, riding orange in the sunset. Snow moves toward Caro in small gray clouds gathering in intensity, casting shadows as they tunnel across the frozen earth. A blaze of snow, and then a young boy hovers above her.

—*Les mauvaises terres,* Caro says to Little Magpie.

He shakes his head and spreads his arms as if to embrace the entire landscape.

—*Paha ska.*

—Of course, she says, White Hills.

The boy descends and kneels beside her. They cut the white sea into a grid of squares, mark off each one with string and wooden stakes, and begin to dig.

12

Alex's bed is empty, the blue-and-white comforter smoothed and the matching pillow shams propped decoratively against the cherrywood headboard. Daniel squeezes his eyes shut, not quite believing she is gone, as if by blinking he can conjure her from air. He opens his eyes, but his daughter, his awkward, exquisite, blonde-haired daughter, has vanished.

Henry's bed is empty as well, the covers askew, the pillow tossed halfway across the room. His son never made his bed, so it is impossible to tell if he had actually slept there before disappearing into thin air. Daniel touches the sheets to see if they are still warm. Cold. How long does it take for sheets to chill after a body has left them?

He pats down his son's bedding, just to be sure, even though the covers cannot possibly hide a two-hundred pound seventeen-year-old. He checks under the bed and finds what he expects, the history books Henry covets—an enormous atlas of Civil War battlefields, books detailing firearms and military strategy and the long history of the United States at war.

He sits down heavily on the edge of his son's bed. What the hell, he thinks, am I going to tell Caro? That I lost the children? It feels as if a weight is pressing on his eyelids from the inside. He falls face first into Henry's mattress and inhales the familiar scent of his son's sweat. "I'll wait, that's all there is to it," he mumbles into the mattress. "I'll wait for my children to reappear."

Then he catches something, a low but unmistakable hum coming through the closed bedroom window. Henry's muffled baritone. Crossing to the window, he squints into the darkness. On the roof of the attached garage are silhouettes of two fragile bodies. Alex and Henry.

He stifles the urge to throw open the window and pull his children inside. Hadn't his son, for all practical purposes a man, long outgrown his childish preoccupation with heights—rooftops, the high dive, the uppermost rung of the tallest playground sliding board? Hadn't his daughter more sense than to perch on a pitched roof a dozen feet above the ground?

Stay cool, he tells himself. Let them see that I've changed.

When the children went through adolescence, they called him "Mother." Mother, Mother, they chorused whenever he crossed the invisible line into overprotection. Caro went along, colluding with her children against him, deluded into thinking the children had a sixth sense about danger. He was the vigilant one, the willing scapegoat for her loose notion of security, the one who saw the lethality of uncovered electrical outlets, Venetian blind cords, Drano. He worked diligently to prevent all possible bad outcomes—outlet covers, cordless roll-up shades, syrup of ipecac. Or was the antidote to Drano milk? He forgets now, just as Caro had a gift for forgetting the near-misses. The evening five-year-old Henry, running from one of Daniel's tirades over something so trivial he could not remember its cause, sailed through the plate glass storm door Daniel had failed to cover with safety stickers, and managed only to slice open his right wrist. Twenty stitches. Or the rushed school morning Alex flipped the family's Volvo station wagon and ended up sandwiched between its crumpled roof and the steering wheel, gashing her forehead but otherwise unhurt. Thirteen stitches. Or the drowsy summer afternoon swarming yellow-jackets left Henry's feet swollen and bruised when he walked barefoot over their underground nest. No stitches, but many tears.

Yes, they'll see that I've changed, even if it means they fall to their deaths.

What am I thinking? That if they survived the fall, they would learn the lessons I've been trying to teach them all their lives? And what were those incontrovertible truths? That everything bad can be prevented with the proper foresight? That every decision must be rational? That being safe is paramount? Stupid, he thinks, even I didn't always follow those rules.

Henry turns toward the window, staring directly at his father, but he does not see him. From the darkened bedroom, however, Daniel can see his son's face clearly. He is ten again, his eyes glazed with excitement, a kind of madness, the summer evening Daniel first discovered him here. And there, scuttling crab-wise across the hot shingles, is he himself, seven years younger, unbothered by the arthritis that now plagues his right knee. He can feel the terror of his former forty-year-old self as he clings to the sharp edges of the shingles, trying to gain a handhold on the crumbling asphalt. Is this the same man who dreamed cities of glass?

"Isn't it awesome?" Henry said. He spread his arms to encompass the twilit sky. "You can see everything from up here."

Daniel was content to see only as far as the carved English boxwood edging the boundary between their backyard and the neighbor's, and even that from the relative safety of his kitchen window. Henry imagined a never-ending universe. Daniel saw then what he sees now: his son's broken body sprawled on the concrete patio twelve feet below.

The vision dissolves when Henry turns from the window without noticing his father spying on them. Daniel takes a deep breath and opens the window, slowly, slowly, so as not to startle them.

"You guys okay?" he asks, straining for just the right note of buoyancy.

Alex rises slightly from her spot on the roof. "Is it Mom?"

"Relax. She's okay, she's sleeping." He sits down on the window sill and swings his legs outside. Still seated, he clings to the solid wooden frame, his feet unevenly but firmly planted on the sloping roof. To his right, the peak of the garage roof looms, its black ridge framed against the navy blue sky. To his left, the roof slants down and away, to the gutter clogged with leaves from the previous autumn. Beyond the eave the backyard gives way to the boxwood hedge and the stand of Norway spruce and Scotch pine foresting the lawn next door. The peak of the nearest neighbor's roof rises darkly between these evergreens.

"Admiring the view?" Henry asks.

"I thought I might."

"It is *some* view," Alex says, smirking.

He sighs. "You two never let up, do you?"

Then he gives in to fate, kneels down on all fours, and begins the long crawl across the roof, keeping his eyes focused on the blanket not ten feet away, where his children wait.

13

It is the darkest of the night, cold and still, an early winter evening on the prairie. A fire blazes in an earthen pit, and all around the fire, Sioux men and women warm their hands and tell stories. The eldest of the men sucks on the end of a long white pipe, then pauses, a thin trail of smoke rising from the bowl. He nods occasionally, murmuring *a-ho, a-ho*, as he listens to one of the tribe's young men, his brother's son with the black hair and the black eyes and the quick smile, recite the story of Thunder-Bird,

—a great black bird with the wings of a vulture and the beak of a hawk. He came, the young man says, once every snow to devour the most beautiful maiden in our village. It was a time of great sorrow when the snows came over the ridge, for the people of the village already mourned the living girl chosen to die.

The storyteller glances at the young woman nursing his tiny infant daughter, who grasps her mother's index finger.

—One winter of the new snow, he continues, a girl that a young man loved very much, the most beautiful of all the girls in the village, was chosen as Thunder-Bird's sacrifice.

His wife looks up at him and smiles. An old woman pauses in her work, stringing bright beads on strands of silken thread, and runs her index finger along the baby's plump cheek. —*Hay*, she says. Yes.

The man goes on. —The thought of his beloved dying in the jaws of the terrible bird grieved the young man. He resolved to go with the girl to meet the monster, protected by the war-shirt the girl had sewn for him and painted with red flying creatures more terrible than Thunder-Bird. Hand-in-hand, they went out to meet the great bird...

Little Magpie nods toward his people. —One of our women has died, he says. —This is how we honor her.

Caro and he are kneeling on the ground, not twenty yards from the fire, surrounded by small mounds of dirt and sod. She rubs the rough patches on her fingers, calluses she had long since forgotten hardened to this new work.

—We, too, honor the dead with stories, Caro says.

The storyteller's voice is caught by a sudden wind that churns through the empty stretch of night and buffets the flames, which leap beyond the confines of the fire pit. Sinuous orange-red tongues twist around the vaporous bodies of the men and women, the young boys and girls. Everyone is clothed in white and flame, languidly shifting shape in the wind. The flames envelop the last of the mourners: the storyteller whose lips still move with the words of the story of the great bird.

The flames swirl back into themselves and die down, and all that remains is a flat expanse of prairie and a small fire that warms Caro and Little Magpie as they work. The boy removes a scab of grass with his trowel. —*That part of Wovoka's vision about the dead returning to us if we danced was what appealed to me. To think I should see my dear mother, grandmother, my brother and sisters again!*

—I know, she says. —I'd like to see the dead again: my parents, my uncles. She scrapes at the dry dirt and sand and scoops the loose earth into a bucket. Someone had promised her clarity before death. Was this the promised clarity?

—*Soon fifty of us, little boys, aged eight to ten, started out across country from the Pine Ridge School, shedding* their *clothes,* their *language, as we traveled. Almost thirty miles we walked. There on Porcupine Creek thousands of Sioux were in the camp, a great fire already blazing.*

—And the people, wearing the sacred shirts and feathers, formed a ring, she says.

The bucket is heavy, filled with their gatherings, and together, they take it to the wooden sifter and dump the contents onto the shallow mesh tray.

—*We boys were in it. All joined hands. Everyone was respectful and quiet, expecting something wonderful to happen.*

The two of them shake the sifter back and forth, pressing clumps of dirt through the sieve. She plucks a small artifact from the mesh, a piece of clouded pale green glass, which reminds her of sea glass formed from an old Coke bottle. The shard has no archaeological value, but it is beautiful, and so she slips it into her pocket.

The fire leaps and burns, leaps and burns. Somewhere in the world, a little boy bored with mathematics class drops his pencil on gray linoleum. It rolls and rolls and rolls without stopping. Little Magpie picks it up and shows it to her. She takes the pencil from him. Was this the promise of death, a number-two pencil sent across time and worn down to the nub?

—*Haŋ*, she says. —Go on.

—*The leaders beat time and sang as the people danced, going round to the left in a sidewise step. Occasionally, someone fell unconscious into the center and lay there "dead." After a while, many lay about in that condition, unable to rise, unable to move. They did not want to move.*

—Because they could see their dear ones.

—*As each one came to, he or she slowly sat up and looked about, bewildered, and then began wailing inconsolably.*

—It's hard to leave the dead, she says. They place the sifter on the ground and return to the work of the square they are excavating.

—Can you hear the others? he asks.

—Always I hear the voices. It's hard to quiet them. She covers her ears, but the voices come from inside her.

—No, Little Magpie says. He pulls her hands down. —Listen to them.

§

The men were separated from the women... and they were surrounded by the soldiers. Then came next the village of the Indians and that was entirely surrounded by the soldiers also. When the firing began, of course the people who were standing immediately around the young man who fired the first shot were killed right together, and then they turned their guns... upon the women who were in the lodges standing there under the flag of truce, and of course as soon as they were fired upon they fled, the men fleeing in one direction and the women running in two different directions....

There was a woman with an infant in her arms who was killed as she almost touched the flag of truce, and the women and children of course were strewn all along the circular village until they were dispatched. Right near the flag of truce a mother was shot down with her infant; the child not knowing that its mother was dead was still nursing, and that especially was a very sad sight. The women as they were fleeing with their babes were killed together, shot right through, and the women who were very heavy with child were also killed. All the Indians fled in these three directions, and after almost all of them had been killed a cry was made that all those who were not killed, wounded should come forth and they would be safe. Little boys who were not wounded came out of their places of refuge, and as soon as they came in sight a number of soldiers surrounded them and butchered them there.

§

I desire to express my admiration of the gallant conduct of my command in an engagement with a band of Indians in desperate condition and crazed by religion.

§

The action of the Commanding Officer, in my judgment at the time... was most reprehensible. The disposition of his troops was such that in firing upon the warriors they fired directly towards their own lines and also into the camp of the women and children. And I have regarded the whole affair as most unjustifiable and worthy of the severest condemnation.

§

That women and children were casualties was unfortunate but unavoidable, and most must have been [killed] from Indian bullets... The Indians at Wounded Knee brought their own destruction as surely as any people ever did. Their attack on the troops was as treacherous as any in the history of Indian warfare, and that they were under a strange religious hallucination is only an explanation and not an excuse.

§

I had not gone far until I met White Face, my wife. She had been shot. She mumbled, "Let me pass. Let me pass. You go on. We will all die soon, but I must get to my mother. There she is."

She crawled to where her mother lay, at the top of the bank, but as she lifted the body in her arms, she fell dead, shot again.

... It comes to me bitterly that perchance there was no Savior for the Sioux, or that the white man's Gods were stronger. Why else did He stand silently, with hidden face, to let His people perish?

§

Little Magpie rises from his kneeling position, continues rising, growing and aging before her eyes. He is ten. He is twelve. He is fourteen. His shoulders broaden, stubble shadows his smooth cheeks. He dusts the white dirt from his breechclout and then looks down at her with liquid brown eyes. They are, she realizes with a shock, Henry's eyes.

—Is it better? he asks. A man now, he extends his hand to her.

—A little, she says. She takes his hand and stands to face him. —White men mistook your reserve for indifference. Worse, insolence.

—We were taught to be quiet by our grandmothers, but we felt the same things all children feel. We loved our parents, we hoped for a better life than theirs. We thought we could live in peace among the Europeans, borrowing what was good in their culture, and even some of what was bad. It was a dream.

—A dream, she repeats. —Is it over?

14

"You look ridiculous," Henry says to his father, who has managed to crawl to within three feet of the safety of the blanket. Daniel pauses to catch his breath, clutching the cutting edges of two asphalt shingles.

"You need help?" Alex asks. She offers him her hand, just out of reach.

"I'm coming, I'm coming," he says. "It's just my knee..."

The excuse sounds lame even to him. He turns his head to the left, a mistake, he realizes too late. The familiar markers on the ground, bushes and small trees he planted with his own hands, are shrinking.

The earth spins too quickly, rotating degree by degree before his eyes. He blinks, and in the time it takes to blink, the earth tilts away from him.

"So you're just going to kneel there all night, old man?" Henry asks. He stands suddenly and mimes a rapper's shuffle.

"You're going to give me a heart attack!" Daniel shouts, letting go one hand and reaching out for his son. Henry defies gravity, spins in place, and then flops down cross-legged on the blanket.

"So this is what you two do when I'm not around?" Daniel hunches over and presses his fingers into his ribcage. "Court certain death?" His heart is beating wildly again, and for the second time that night, he wonders if he is having a heart attack.

"Are you all right?" Alex asks.

He takes a deep breath. "Yeah, yeah, I'm fine."

His heart skips another beat, and then another, and then it resumes its usual rhythm. Amazing what the heart can endure, he thinks. It can inflict its own pain and go on beating. It can witness someone it loves waste to nothing, scream over the merest touch, vomit every good thing. It can watch the veins burn, the skin swell and burst, the bones dissolve—and still it beats, beats, beats. A spineless, indifferent muscle, the heart.

He lets go of the shingles and sits down next to Alex. "Humor your old man. Just stay earthbound while I'm out here?"

"Okay, *Mother*," Henry says.

Alex draws her hand across her stomach, a private signal between them. They have a language of coughs, hand motions, eyerolls. This one means, no doubt, take it easy on Dad. Henry looks down at his hands, raises his right to his mouth, and chews on his fingernails.

"We couldn't sleep," Alex says.

"That makes three of us," Daniel says, and removes his son's hand from his mouth.

"Is it safe to leave Mom alone?" Alex asks.

He wonders if she ever stops thinking about it, her mother dying. During the first week of February, when the doctors gave Caro four to six weeks, Alex immediately abandoned her second semester of sophomore year at Columbia and came home. Caro had outlasted the most optimistic end of that prediction by two weeks.

"She's *fine*," he says, a little too sharply. Henry resumes his nail-biting, methodically tearing away a hangnail with his teeth.

"She's fine for now," Daniel says more quietly. He resists the urge to pull Henry's hand from his mouth again, and leans back on the slanting shingles as casually as he dares, feigning nonchalance. Above him billowy blue-white clouds move through the navy sky; the moon, hidden behind one, illuminates its periphery in a bright white glow. The moon glides across the cloud, brightening first one edge, then the middle, and then the other edge before appearing briefly between clouds and disappearing behind the next.

This is not the world in which his wife is dying. Maybe that is why the kids are out here. Even forcing the sentences to form in his head—Caro is dying, Caro will die, tomorrow or the day after, you'll wake up and she'll be gone—none of these made her coming death any more real.

"Full moon," Alex says, following her father's gaze skyward.

"It's supposed to make people crazy," Henry says. He howls, the vibration of it echoing in Daniel's spine.

Alex punches Henry lightly on the arm. "Stop it! You'll wake the dead." She covers her mouth. "I'm sorry, Dad. I didn't mean—"

"Don't sweat it." He hugs her to him. "It's funny how many expressions we have like that. You wouldn't believe how often people apologize to me. 'You scared me to death.' 'You'll catch your death.' 'Cold as death.'"

"Nothing is certain but death and taxes?"

"That's deep, Henry. How about 'O death, where is thy sting? O grave, where is thy victory?'" Alex says.

"'Though I walk through the valley of the shadow of death, I will fear no evil. Surely goodness and mercy shall follow me all the days of my life,'" Daniel says.

"Mercy?" Henry says quietly. "That's a joke."

"Henry."

"Deny it, Dad."

The two stare at each other across the short distance separating them. He's right, Daniel thinks. But blaming God or believing in miracles only makes him feel worse.

"'Death is the mother of beauty; hence from her, alone, shall come fulfillment to our dreams and our desires.'" Alex shakes her head. "That was one of Mom's favorites."

Was, Daniel thinks.

"Where's it from?" Henry asks.

"'Sunday Morning.' Wallace Stevens," Alex says. "Really, dawg, you should read."

"I read."

"*The Essential Calvin and Hobbes* doesn't qualify as literature, stupid."

"*Dad . . .* "

Daniel shakes his head. "Someday the two of you will be all you have."

"Orphans, you mean?"

"I mean that you should be kind to each other. I'm not going anywhere." Dumb, he thinks, just let them talk.

"So what did that hospice woman have to say this morning?" Alex asks, glancing at Henry.

Up to now, Caro and he have been honest with the children. What the hospice nurse had told him was, "Within the week." Just like that, as she was leaving.

"Nothing's changed. She said there's no way to be sure." That was the problem with this dying. He had not expected the process would be so relentless, the body failing, not organ by organ, but seemingly everything at once. The cancer spread from breast to bone to blood, yet the body hung on. It clung. It refashioned itself into an unrecognizable other that would be with them at the final moment.

Henry shakes his head back and forth. "Why Mom?"

Daniel shrugs. "We've been through this, Henry."

"'There are worse things waiting for men than death,'" Alex says.

"That's comforting, *ancient half-sister*," Henry says. "Roald Dahl, in case you're wondering."

"Gobstoppers," she replies, and sticks out her tongue.

"Oompa-loompas," Daniel adds, squeezing his son's shoulder. "It *is* peaceful up here, kids. If you forget that 144 square feet of concrete lurk below."

"All together, this has been such a cheerful conversation," Alex says.

She is looking up, not down, and if he does the same, he sees that he is sitting with his grown children, nothing more, nothing less. How quickly life changes. One minute, they are teething on silver trainer cups, the next, chewing their nails to stubs. One minute, they are crying over a lost and precious skeleton key, the next, someone is calling from the hospital to say there's been an accident, your daughter's hurt. And then there is the lump, no larger than a lima bean (the doctor's very words), and then the breast is gone.

Daniel watches the moon pass through a small cloud and emerge into a clear patch of navy, its white face cast with blue shadows. He howls—aah-ooo—a single soft blues note, the "ooo" pitched high and then cut off in a low strangled scream. The strange screech carries outward into the deep wall of blue and dies away. Henry glances at his father, and then, as if on cue, the two sing softly together—Aah-oooooo, aah-aah-oooooo. Their howls echo and die.

Daniel turns to Alex. She looks neither happy nor sad as she stands, higher up along the slope of the roof so that she looks ten feet tall. She raises her arms to the sky in a V and throws back her head, the pale skin of her long neck and the fall of her blonde hair catching the moonlight, glowing white. She opens her mouth wide and takes several deep breaths, her chest rising and falling, rising and falling in the shadows.

Henry leans over and whispers to his father, "She's gone mad."

"I'm mad, you're mad, we're all mad here," Alex says, her voice carrying upward into the darkness. She takes one more deep breath and then exhales a long, low O that turns into an "ooo" that continues for what feels like minutes as the breath leaves her body.

They listen to the fading echo. When it finally dies, she looks down on them and smiles.

"Beat that, boys," she says.

15

Bones float in a sea a thousand thousand shades of white. A woman's pelvis materializes in the white before her, the bone's surface marked by the ridges of childbirth.

Mother, Caro thinks. Mother.

Above the pelvis, ribs form one by one out of air, and then four chambers fashion themselves into a heart, and the heart thumps softly in its cage. Long bones of the legs, femur and tibia, issue from the pelvis, lengthening until they touch the ground. And then the bones of the arms appear, humerus and radius and ulna, and the small bones of the hands and feet, the metacarpals and the metatarsals. Vertebrae assemble themselves into an undulant cord, and next a skull emerges, it too from air, a skull and a soft tongue, and the irises leach color from the black of the pupils, and flesh like light envelops the bones.

The Miniconjou Sioux mother stands before her, clothed in white. She can hear the woman's heart beating through the bones and the skin, and her own heart beating, vibrating in the pulse of her neck, and soon two voices join, the mother's voice and hers, in the dust of the tent where she sleeps in the white sea.

—Mother, is that you?

—*Haŋ le miye što.* Yes, this is me. She floats above Caro, and everything is white. They are together, nowhere and everywhere at once.

—Tell me what you've come to tell me.

—We believed, she begins, that if our white robes caught the fire of the dance, the dead would return to us. We were promised rain, and rain came. We were promised snow, and that, too, came. We had almost touched the flag of truce flying from the great tree when the guns blazed. I was unconscious, for how long I do not know. Then I came to, and everyone was bleeding. I saw a dead mother, her son still nursing. My own son was shot but he lived for a time. He lived through Wounded Knee.

Mother pauses to adjust the folds of her robes, and her body, ethereal as fog rising from thawing earth, wavers on a current of air.

—I carried him, still breathing, toward the Stronghold where I thought he would be safe. My son was shot, bullets through his braids, through his skull, and out of his mouth. He spoke bullets, and then he died.

She bows her head briefly and then raises it. White, white, everything so white.

—What could I do, Caro? Leave him alone to freeze in the wind and the white? No. I removed a bullet from his hair and braided it again. I wiped the blood from his face. And then I sang to him. I sang to him in the snow coming over the ridge, in the sun coming over the snow. I sang to him of the bones of the giants coming over the snow, of the moonrise and the stars and the sun. All coming over the snow. I sang to him so he would not be lonely for his mother when he finally left this earth. My song was a happy one, for I knew it would not be long before we were together again. When I died, I felt my body lifted up into the sky with the moon and the stars and my son. There was no fire. Were the chiefs wrong to wish fire over the earth for our people's sake? Was that our sin?

16

For the third time that night, Daniel stands at the bathroom sink preparing for bed, washing his face, brushing his teeth, his children safely asleep. It had been a long time, too long, since he had last tucked them in and kissed them goodnight and wished them pleasant dreams. Sliding his toothbrush into its holder, he has the wild hope that these rituals will return the night to an easeful passage and usher in several hours of uninterrupted sleep.

And then he hears Caro calling, "Daniel, please."

He finds her thrashing in the bed, the blankets bunched at her feet, the damp white sheet twisted loosely around her body.

"Get them away from me," she says, and tears at the sheet.

He climbs into the bed, wrestles the sheet from her body, and throws it on the floor. She is shivering, or shaking, cold or in pain, he does not know which.

"Help me, help me, help me."

"Caro, Caro, Caro," he whispers, and pulls a blanket over both of them.

Lord, let this be over, he thinks. Then *No*.

Restless, she presses her back into his chest, taking shallow, strained breaths. He hugs her as tight as he dares, thinking of her frail spine. It soothes her to be held as if bound in a cocoon, as if their two bodies are one. They lie like this for what seems like an hour, Daniel trying to breathe for his wife.

Her voice, hoarse and deep, a voice not her own, startles him. "The giants... are returning."

"The giants?"

"Mammoth... and buffalo... coming over... the ridge... in a snowstorm... do you... see them?" she asks, the phrases parsed by her gasping.

He reaches for the button on her morphine pump.

"Don't," she says, slapping his hand away.

"The nurse said—"

"I feel... sick... too much." She stiffens in his arms. "Rub my back."

He strokes her scalp, runs his right hand gently down her neck, and kneads the lump at the top of her spine. She is shaking again in an effort to stave off the pain. Just this morning the hospice nurse had increased the dosage limit on the pump. The hallucinations and the nausea were always worse on these days, but the pain was usually manageable. What is happening inside her, he wonders, to cause so much pain tonight? He imagines the bones ulcerating, the tumors pressing on the nerves of her spinal column, or one of the many internal scars tearing inside her.

The nurse told him, "Don't let her suffer. Use the morphine—the pump, the injectors for breakthrough pain if things become unbearable."

She resists, because no matter what the nurses and the doctors say, she is convinced that too much morphine will only hasten her passage into the twilight sleep that will be the same as death.

After a time, her breathing settles into a more even rhythm.

"Better?" he asks, loosening his grip.

At first she seems to have fallen asleep. Then a low hum comes from deep inside her, followed by soft chanting. "*Ee-nah, hay coo-e-yay. Ee-nah, hay coo-e-yay.*"

"*Ee-nah?*" Daniel asks.

"Mother, come back. Mother, come back."

"Of course," he says. "One of the Ghost Dance songs."

"My brother is crying for you. The buffalo will return if we dance."

"I see them, Caro."

"Coming over the ridge in a snowstorm." She turns toward him, still wrapped in his arms. "Mother, hand me my sharp knife."

"Hand me my sharp knife," he says.

"The buffalo have returned. My father says so." She pulls him close and whispers in his ear, "Promise me you'll tell no one."

"I promise."

§

—Tell no one, Dietrich says. They kneel facing each other and sweep away with their hands the outlines of their bodies in the trench where they made love.

—But we've disturbed the site. She repositions the handful of bison bones on the dirt, but she can only guess how they had lain. She remembers a cluster of shards near the edge of the trench, the rest scattered across its floor.

—A hundred years ago, someone tore the meat from this bone with his teeth and threw it on the ground. Like this. He takes one of the bones and tosses it on the dirt. —For God's sake, ants bring mammal's teeth to their hills to be buried.

—I know all about bioturbation. She picks up the discarded bone and places it with several others in a small pile by her knees.

He shakes his head. —Then you know nothing remains undisturbed forever. Maybe it's as poor, discredited Lamarck proposed: the desires of *animals* direct the force of evolution.

—*Our* desires, she says, are insignificant in the face of nature's.

—Depressions in the earth signify the corruptions of man.

—The carvings on rock are signs of long-vanished streams.

—Honestly, dear girl, you were my most *promising* student. He spreads a canvas tarp on the grass next to the trench. —Come, he says, more gently. —Lie down with me.

He is as old as her father, yet she hesitates only to finish arranging the bones before settling down with him face to face. They are sheltered by the canopy of the white tent, the tent flap beating rhythmically against the canvas wall. She can hear it still, the drumming of the tent flap, and Dietrich's voice.

—We dig where there are signs of life. He runs his tongue along the tip of her right breast. —We've eaten the fruit. We can't go back.

She rolls onto her back and asks, —Who are you?

He traces the blossoming bruise on her breast with his fingertips. She feels tenderness and pain. The breast is whole, smooth, firm under the weight, the heat of his hand.

—Who are you? she repeats, and presses his hand to her breast.

—I'm your father, he says.

—My father is an honorable man.

—Is this honor, he says, touching the tiny diamond of her engagement ring, anything like your love?

He removes his hand from her breast, her breast in his hand, the breast dissolving in his hand.

§

She wakes, screaming. She stares at the morphine tube running into her side as if she has only just now discovered herself hooked up to it, and then wraps the tube once around her hand and yanks at it. Daniel grabs her arm and pins it to the mattress. In response she jabs her free elbow into his ribs. The unexpected pain stops his breath, causing him to loosen his grip on her for a moment before redoubling his efforts, wrapping his arms around her, and squeezing as tight as he can.

Spine, break, paralysis, he thinks. "Stop! Stop! Stop!"

She is stronger than he imagines a woman composed of bones and skin could be. Sweating from the effort to restrain her, he can feel her weakening in his grasp.

"Stop," he says again. "You'll hurt yourself."

She goes limp in his arms, crying now. "Who c-c-c-cares?" she says between hiccups of breath.

"I do," he says. "I do."

"L-l-let me g-go."

"The tube stays in?"

"I p-promise."

He releases her, and she rolls away from him. She is having trouble catching her breath. Audible respiration, he thinks as he listens to her breath pass noisily through her windpipe. Or is it just the mucus from her crying?

"You don't want to talk about it?"

"No," she mumbles into her pillow. "It was just another nightmare."

"Wouldn't it help—"

"No!"

He slides toward her on the bed. "Here, let me check the tube."

"Get away from me." She wards him off with her hand, kneels suddenly, pulls off her nightgown. "See," she says, and tugs on the tube, "still there. See," she says, pointing to her chest, "still gone."

She plants her thumb on the pump's button and pushes it roughly. "Isn't this what you want?" She presses the button again and again. "This is what you want. Say it! Say it!"

Yes, he thinks, let's put an end to this. He watches her, knowing the pump will only deliver so much morphine at one time.

She stops abruptly, covers her face with her hands, and rocks on her knees. "Damn, damn, damn."

Kneeling, he crawls toward her and takes her in his arms. "It's okay, sweetheart."

She brings her arms around his waist. "For-give me." Her speech is slow, her vowels thick and clotted.

"For what? Being angry?" he says. "I'm angry, too."

She looks at him then, pats his cheek. "I'm tired," she says. "Read to me?"

He pulls a clean, dry nightgown over her head and settles her into bed. From the clutter of the nightstand he picks up the yellowed magazine page that contains "'My Soul Is a Light Housekeeper.'" It had been buried beneath the sports schedules and appointment cards and family snapshots on the refrigerator door until she rediscovered it there the week before.

"Imagine," he says, looking straight at her, not the poem in his hand, "'imagine...you could have seen that side of me at the beginning, when we walked for hours along the shore, and you were so certain I was yours just because you loved me...'"

§

She allows herself to be seduced by the words. Imagine. Beginning. Love.

Words. *Ces mauvaises terres.* These bad lands have been crossed before. December night, a hundred years gone. Ghost dancers spinning in the firelight, their faces painted red with crescents and crosses, hands joined knuckle to knuckle. They dance round and round the sacred tree of peace, crossing borders between living and dying, their bodies more beautiful neither living nor dead, their white shirts blackened with magpies to protect them from the bullets. The birds' beating wings lift them into the sky. The dead rise from the earth as the living turn, faster and faster, the earth re-formed beneath them, and when they alight, it is a new earth they come down upon.

For a moment, Caro feels light, light as a dancer, light as love.

The world below is on fire, her spine consumed by flames. She reaches for the button of her crystal dreams, but they are not there. They are here.

§

Dietrich holds up the crooked bit of pipe. The pipe translucent in the light.

The tent flap beating time to some far ago. The dancing has begun, down by the Cheyenne, out on the sacred lands. The white shirts painted, black magpies to stop the bullets. They believe.

—'Mother, the buffalo will return if we dance.' The chiefs beat time and sing.

—A chant, a war cry!

—'Mother, hand me my sharp knife, / Mother, hand me my sharp knife.'

—Fire! Fire on them!

—Should we blame him?

—Yes, all of them. Trade them, blow for blow.

Only bone is shaded with life, translucent in the light. —Not pipe, Dietrich, and please, your hand on my calf?

The bone in the light, a tiny bit of thumb, a child's bone. A little boy alone near the cliff of the Stronghold?

—They're dying, Dietrich.

—There's nothing we can do, dear girl.

So the boy dies alone in the long valley of snow, the tent flap flapping, beating, beating.

— 'Mother, hand me my sharp knife, / Mother, hand me my sharp knife, / Here come the buffalo returning— / Mother, hand me my sharp knife.'

And the boy reduced to bone. The little boy's bone and I am a mother. Henry and Alexandra, their names dissolving in the dust of the Badlands, their bones in my hands, Dietrich's hand on my knee. Is it to be a different story? No. The story is the bones. The tent flap beating, dust rising from the books, words rising in the dust of the ancient books. Do no harm. Do not lie. Do right always.

Language bears the burden of the sacred.

— 'Mother, hand me my sharp knife, / Mother, come back! / Mother, come back!'

Ee-nah, ee-nah. The little boy's mother. Where is she? In the pile of bison bones.

—There is something we can do, Dietrich.

More bones held up to the light, each bone held up to the light.

—Bison. Bison. Bison.

—Sioux garbage, dear girl. The hair curling in his nose.

—Hand me my sharp knife. *Ces mauvaises terres* I still must cross. Where are these lands?

—Here, dear girl.

His hand on my thigh. The children disappear. What have I done?

—Oh, Alex, oh, Henry.

—Your hands are cold, Mother.

—Your hands are cold, Alex.

—'Mother, do come back! My brother is crying for you.'

—Take care of Henry for me.

—Take care of him yourself.

—Please, Alex. Take care of Henry. Take care of Dad.

—What about me, Mother?

—Take care of yourself, too, Alex. A hand in mine. My daughter's? —Yes, above all, take care of yourself.

Bones shine in the light. One by one in the light. Bison. Bison. Bison. Maybe Dietrich is right. A tiny shard of clay pipe. Sioux garbage. Bison. Bison. Human. A pelvis. A skull bone. So the story begins.

Once upon a time, there was a mother and child...

—*Misunkala cheyaya omaniye*. 'My little brother is crying for you— / My father says so!' All ghost dancers all ghosts now, they begin to dance the dance again, in firelight, in white shirts, while little boys play in the dirt, leap frog and bucking horse.

Their shirts protect them. The bullets pass through their braids, all those little children with their bodies in pieces, their braids full of bullets.

—'Mother, hand me my knife!'

—No, dear son, the magpie will protect you.

I rise from bones and the dust and the dance, rise above the earth, above Dietrich above me, the safety of Daniel, of children, my children. Here they are. They are here.

— 'Mother, do come back! My father says so.'

—Your shirts will protect you when I'm gone.

I hold up three bones. Name them as I named my own children. Little Magpie. Mother Magpie. Sacred relics, bones and names. Bullets in their braids, their bones frozen to the earth.

—Let them go, dear girl.

—I *will* bury them.

—Do you want to stay with me or not?

17

Caro awakens just before dawn to Daniel's urgent voice. "Break, break, break," he says, his eyes closed, his breathing steady.

"'At the foot of thy crags, O Sea,'" she whispers, and kisses him on the cheek. "'But the tender grace of a day that is dead will never come back to me.'"

She slides silently to the edge of the bed, places one foot on the floor and then the other, and tests her body for pain, for its ability to hold her up. The pain has subsided, and the worst of the night has passed. Maybe it was not the end, as she had thought, just one of the bad days. The floor feels solid, level, not canting away from her as it has seemed of late, like the floor in a funhouse. Her spine tingles but does not burn, and she can walk, as long as she glides like an ice skater.

A reprieve, she thinks, and tucks the covers under her pillow. Soon I won't even be able to do these small things.

Shuffling down the hallway, she is so familiar with its lines and angles that she does not need to turn on lights. A pale glow is beginning to filter through the house, the lightening before dawn, and that is enough. She pauses at the end of the gallery of pictures in the hall, the shrine she and Daniel have made to their children documenting every year of their lives. Before her is the first photo ever taken of Alex holding Henry in her lap. Sitting in a child-sized wooden rocker, she grasps her baby brother across his tiny chest, the expression on her face full of an ambivalence that asks, Should I drop him now or hold onto him forever? She was fond of telling her parents that she would have been a perfect only child.

Alex *was* the greater miracle, coming after the two failed pregnancies. Caro was not conscious for her birth, a caesarean. Coming out of the black tunnel of anesthesia and into the blinding fluorescent of the hospital recovery room, she remembers Alex's lusty screams and her milk letting down. The two moments could not have happened simultaneously; in her memory they are inextricably linked.

But perhaps because Henry had been born prematurely, an emergency C-section, Caro had felt something different for him than Alex: not a greater love, exactly, but a greater tenderness. In the hospital's neonatal intensive care unit—surrounded by the constant thrum of the ventilators, and the piercing scream of monitors tripped by readings outside the range of normal, and warming beds and incubators each containing a newborn more fragile than Henry—she nursed her tiny son, naked except for a diaper, electrodes attached to wires to monitor God-knows-what snaking from his chest, clear tubes for oxygen slipped up his nose, and a catheter for antibiotics taped to his arm. After the nurses untethered him from the machines and the IVs two weeks after his birth, she had the illogical conviction that nothing bad would ever happen to him again. And nothing had. Did she believe in his safety because he was a boy? How much teasing Daniel had endured over the years, if only for his level-headedness.

Oddly, Alex was more self-sufficient, resilient, with the preternatural calm of one born to endure. Henry was the nail-biter, the nervous twitcher, dweller in silent, rooftop worlds. He required more tenderness. Yes, that was what she would tell Alex before she died: "Be tender toward Henry." It was a small measure of what she had accomplished that her daughter would listen to her.

But what of Daniel? Would Alex's tenderness be enough for him? What were her feelings for Daniel after all these years? He used her, the family, as a buffer for his lost dreams, and that was fine. After all, what were the chances that he would ever have realized his marvelous cities of glass? Yet she recalls finding a newspaper article circled in red—was it 2000, 2001? Could four years have passed since then? "Japanese Firm Awarded Design for All-Glass Pavilion," the headline read. Sanaa was the firm's name, a woman the project's lead architect. The building was to house the Toledo Art Museum's extensive glass collection. It was not a city, just a single building, but it was something he had conceived twenty-five years ago. What had caused him to circle the article and leave it lying around, not saying a word, for her to see? She had thrown it away.

During their very first conversation in the basement of Canaday Library, Daniel had spoken of his belief that glass architecture could change the way people lived. Social transparency, he called it. An elimination of the class system. Even in her youthful idealism, she had thought these goals far-fetched; in fact, she thought it equally likely that such architecture would transform society into a police state.

But the sketches he showed her—those were incredible. She still found his drawings in odd places, in the margins of magazines, on crumpled tissues and paper napkins. She had stolen one of a glass cathedral, Daniel's paean to Taut's *Cathedral in the Rocks*, but his was even more elaborate. An intricate web of glass resolved into prismatic domes and cupolas, which reflected and refracted the sun like kaleidoscopes. Yes, breathtaking the design was, and safe, hers, slipped between the pages of an old college notebook. When he had searched for the drawing several years before, she had thought of it there, nestled among her own sketches of cutting flake and bones.

Was she to blame for steering him toward a more sensible application of his architectural talents? His houses were marvels of design that naturally inhabited the colors with which they were saturated: a steel-gray house bathed to a rich blue by an open expanse of sky, or a pale yellow residence burnished to gold by a peculiar slant of the autumn sun, or a dwelling of burnt sienna dappled darker with shadows cast by an ancient oak. His clients dwelled in the more exclusive Philadelphia Main Line enclaves and in the compact duplexes hard by the Paoli Local. He had followed Taut's career trajectory from utopian glass to practical paint. His reputation was made on the basis of these houses—he had developed a cult of believers in the possibilities of color—and he seemed satisfied.

A good husband. That is what her mother had called him. And he *was* good. He had supported her decision to quit her job teaching high school anthropology to raise Alex, even though it meant the family had to struggle for several years on one salary. He had dreams, and then he became a realist. When exactly had that change occurred? She could not pinpoint the moment one thing became another.

He loved her. That she knew. He had told her many times, before the cancer, that his heart still raced when he saw her, just as it had raced the night he spied on her in the library, and the night she danced her spectral dance and consummated their love. Consummate: a grandiose word for the awkward groping and unsyncopated rhythm of their first sex.

He had told her more than once that he was glad they had waited. Had he been fooled by the white nightgown, the lie of the wedding night dance? So easy it was to turn and turn and catch his heart in its beat, beating. What had made her dance that night? Was it the nightgown with its sumptuous yards of white chiffon edged with voluptuous lace? She felt pure again as it slipped down the length of her body that night, slipped down and washed her clean of Dietrich. Had she betrayed herself to Daniel in her recent, half-remembered hallucinations? Would he tell her if he knew?

That was not the problem, was it? She tried to remember the last time her own heart raced at the prospect of seeing Daniel, though the fact of it did not divide her life cleanly into before and after. It was, rather, a gradual wearing-away of the most intense feeling. She had loved him, she still loved him, she loved the way their bodies often rhymed, but she did not long for him in the middle of her days, and for that she felt she had again betrayed him. Somehow this betrayal seemed like the larger one. Not saying, as she might have, that she still felt the same way. What was the harm of a lie, a little white lie, to spare his feelings?

Rather than deny love, she simply said nothing, let him hug her in his tentative way, still hoping that she would reciprocate someday, reclaim what had been merely misplaced. She had not lied, not about love, but it was a lie nonetheless. Would it have mattered if she had simply said, "I know exactly how you feel," and let him think she meant *still*, not *past*, the feeling of too-much Tab and giddy intimacies and the first, brief tongue-kiss against the carrels? With a half-life akin to uranium, the saccharine scientists had later discovered caused cancer in laboratory rats still coursed through her body, eating holes in her spine, filling her lymph nodes with so much fluid that the skin tore and leaked. Daniel patiently cleaned it all— the vomited pills and the sweat and the seeping lymphatic fluid—changed the pads under her legs and her nightdress even as she slept in it. When he saw her now, hairless and bloated, her dark brown eyes dulled almost gray, her skin the color of ash and peeling away in sheets, did his breath still go all thin and papery at the sight of her? How hard would it have been to pretend that she loved him exactly the same?

She pours herself a half-glass of red zinfandel, her favorite wine, strictly forbidden by her doctors, something she will not be able to keep down. Her weakened eyes cannot quite make out the tiny scroll of warnings on the label. They have to do with pregnancy and nursing, she had read them many times when she was well, before tamoxifen and exemestane, paclitaxel and vinorelbine, docetaxel and capecitabine. It used to take her days to learn each new drug's name.

The wine stings her tongue, burns slightly as it slips down her esophagus. Closing her eyes, she waits for the alcohol to cross into the bloodstream, for the conversion of burning to lightness. She takes another sip and scans the clutter on the refrigerator door, the layers accumulating without her attention to this small detail of their lives. Mostly there are bills covered in Daniel's red scrawl, procedures rejected by their insurance company for which he needs to follow up. She thinks of the hours she spent on the bills in the early phases of her treatment, before the numbers and the procedures jumbled together in her mind and she could not concentrate long enough to make sense of the muddle. She riffles the pages of one bill whose unreimbursed expenses total $32,000. At least they could afford the best care.

That frail girl, she thinks. There is the young woman—twenty or forty, hard to tell which—her skin tinged yellowish-blue from chemotherapy. She is shuffling down the center hallway, pushing her own chrome IV stand. Hello, little girl, what happened to you? Her mother is there, worrying a damp tissue to shreds. You know, she says to Caro, the HMO refused to cover the bone marrow transplant. Said it was experimental for her type of leukemia. Said they were very sorry. Said there was nothing they could do.

The girl walks right through Caro and into the family room. She turns and waves and then continues her painful shuffle through the stone fireplace and out into the night.

Caro closes her eyes. Do you have children? the mother's voice says, and then it, too, fades. She opens her eyes. Moonlight falls through the family room skylights, imbuing the space with blue-violet light. Except for the light, the room is empty. She follows the path the girl took and crosses to her favorite chair, the cabbage rose brocade her mother willed her. Holding her glass of forbidden wine, she settles into the depressions of the faded cushions, into the imprint of her mother's body, a body she remembers for its almost impossible softness, and the consolation of that softness. She takes a sip of wine, savors it for a moment, and then places the glass amid the clutter on the side table. How many times had her mother held her in this very chair when she was little, talking to her or reading to her or simply sitting quietly? How many times had her mother rested here alone? Like her mother, Caro loved to sit here in the early morning hours, writing in her notebooks or just dozing, before the family began making its demands on her.

From the pocket of her robe she pulls the housekeeping poem that perfectly captures the unidentifiable yearning she has felt throughout her marriage, the doubts she has had about love's possibilities and fulfillments, the certainties about its potential for devastation, bound always to absence. How did the poet, a man named Lawrence Raab, inhabit so precisely a woman's voice? Her voice. "'My Soul Is a Light Housekeeper,'" she mouths to herself, and then the parenthetical note: "Error in the printing of the line 'my soul is a lighthouse keeper,' by an unknown female poet." This poem sparked by chance, a simple misprint.

So much is left to chance, she thinks. Where was that line from?

She closes her eyes and concentrates, sees on blue-lined notebook paper the blurred words of a poem she had labored over not long before the onset of her illness, "The Collapse of Distance" scrawled in oversized, neat cursive across the white margin at the top of the page. Then the opening stanzas come into focus:

> So much is left to chance—the cleft of a chin
> or the Moon, stars born we see
> only after they've begun to die.
>
> If the Moon had spun another quarter turn
> before locking into the tug of Earth,
> as all things are ultimately bound one to another,
>
> and, facing us, we had not a Man, but a single eye
> focused inward, would distance have transformed
> itself into something comprehensible?
>
> And if…and if…the universe succumbs…

She sighs. It feels as if a black felt eraser has smudged her thoughts or a fog like steel wool has descended. The rest of the poem is in her notebooks somewhere, and she could find it if she wanted. She does not want to.

She skims the Raab poem on the torn page in front of her until she reaches the lines Daniel never reads to her.

> *...Imagine, love,*
> *the tedium of this watch. On almost every day*
> *nothing happens.*

Why does he skip those words? Does he think her life, circumscribed by children and marriage, is filled with regret?

The tedium of this watch: he is watching her, waiting for the final moment: the instant she crosses over. She has come to believe that the line is not as clear as he supposes. Does he know that she would not blame him if he wished her to die soon? A day or week, more or less, what would it matter? Some days she feels that the fight is over, and then she remembers the children. So much is left to chance.

Even archaeology she had chosen on a whim, captivated by Dietrich and his passion for finding the Paleo-Americans. On the first day of class in her junior year, he had paced back and forth in front of her, on the raised platform of the lecture hall, elegant and inaccessible in his rumpled white button-down and his straight-cut Levis, his hair a silvery-gray and his lined face ruddy and thick-skinned from years spent outdoors. Right then, watching him speak with such passion about his quest for the first Americans, she had decided to follow him. She would not settle, as her mother had, for marriage and children. She would travel. She would dig. Instead she was startled by the sudden percussion of falling books and Daniel sorting them into piles according to the numbers on the spines. How different life might have been but for that rack of falling books. Every moment spawned by that moment, the future and the past. Could the future create the past? What was she thinking? Maybe that was just the morphine speaking to her in its dual language of clarity and obscurity.

> *...And isn't it wrong to yearn*
> *for a great storm just to feel important?*

Here was their storm, in the middle of their lives. But was the potential for this devastation not always inside her?

> *Imagine you could have seen that side of me*
> *at the beginning...*

Every side at once.

> *...but understand, dear, it wasn't such a great*
> *change.*

She places the poem on the side table among the photos and the books. Moonlight creases the slight shadow in the crook of her elbow and turns the outer layers of her skin translucent. She lifts her arm into the moonlight, fingering the blue tracery of the vein that runs from her hand, across her wrist, and down her forearm. She can see the morphine, shards of crystal, coursing with her blood through her veins. The skin peels back until it is just this blue vein, like a pulsing thread, alive with blood. She knows it will not be long until everything is a dream. She drifts in and out of sleep on her mother's chair, thinking of Daniel without skin, how she could know every part of him, his bones and his breath, the closed map of his circulatory system, the direction of his heart.

18

The missing beats of her breath, so much like the caw-caw-caw of the crow outside the picture window, awaken him. He has over the years gotten used to waking alone in the early morning hours only to find her gone, gone for a walk in the first light of dawn, or more frequently, gone to doze in her mother's chair by the family room fireplace.

The night's karma has been the empty bed, first his children's, now hers, the covers folded neatly under her pillow, as if she had never been there, as if the night had never happened.

So she felt well enough to make the bed, he thinks. Last night was not the last night, just another long night.

Before they had finally fallen asleep, he had touched his fingers to her cheek, let them slide down the length of her long slow neck, across the strong bone of her clavicle, around the supple curve of her shoulder. She was there only minutes ago (wasn't she?) in sleep borne upon the strength of his voice and the words she wanted to hear. He buries his face in her pillow, in the impression left by her shoulder.

So this is how it will be. He pulls the pillow lengthwise to his chest and breathes in the scent of Dove soap and the faint metallic odor of her sweat. The worry of her leaving him, like the terrible conviction of a nightmare in the first moments of wakefulness, will no longer haunt him. It makes his pain easier to bear, to find only one thing missing at a time, one thing and then the next, until, he imagines, there is nothing left.

The thought that she will be with him until she is gone, and the pillow's softness, and the lingering vestiges of her body, lull him back to sleep.

§

He sees himself, fully clothed in a navy blue suit, starched white shirt, and red tie, sitting cross-legged in a scorched field of grass. The sun is directly overhead, burning his scalp along the part of his hair, and he is sweating. In his lap are government forms, before him a committee of men and women, just heads with eyes peering at him over reading glasses.

—What is your name? they say in unison.

—Daniel Singleman.

—What is your age?

—23.

—What is your occupation?

—I'm currently working on a master's degree in architecture.

—What is the purpose of your project?

—I envision forty-nine tall glass rectangles, arranged in a grid seven times seven, towering in this empty field, a city of glass to honor the known dead, the missing, and the dead disappeared and never to be found. A new form of the city is what I propose, one that will transform individual loss into the possibility of collective renewal and signify a transformation away from man's long history of using catastrophe to effect change.

The disembodied heads wag back and forth—how can this be? a city of glass? is it possible? they murmur to one another—and then they dissolve into swirls of dust that resolve into glass tombstones rising one by one as if sprouting from the earth, a city of nameless dead. Through these sheets of glass streams bright sunlight. Blinded, he squeezes his eyes to shut out the light. Then the shattering. Glass slabs fall like dominoes, one into the next, and the sun is gone, and it is raining crystal, and out of the crystal rain rises a massive granite wall of names, a continuous wall of names, a great V of black slashing through the earth. Maya Lin's vision: cut the earth and let it heal over. A raised and visible scar. His classmate Maya, lovely Maya, stands before the wall incanting the chiseled names that run along its surface and blur at the edges, and then the letters leap off the granite and rearrange themselves into new names. He recognizes the names. They are his clients. Maya turns to wave at him (she'd been a friend years ago), turns to him and waves and even mouths, Hello there, Daniel, before her face reshapes itself into the face of his most recent customer, a Main Line woman who had insisted on red stucco. She stands in front of him, her body sheathed in a red silk Chanel suit, but no, her face is that of his first-grade teacher, who wags a wooden ruler at him.

—I want the color of blood, she tells him, not cardinals. You simply have to make it less red. And whatever you do, you must stay inside the lines.

—Houses fall, red or blue, he says. —Someday you will not be here.

—Get out, she says, pointing the ruler at him and then at the long bank of classroom windows. —Go!

Suddenly he is on a ladder that stretches into the sky. Choking in a torrent of red rain, he rouses himself to semi-wakefulness and finds the sheets tangled around him. They are bathed in his own sweat.

"Maya Lin," he says aloud.

19

The weight of Caro's body presses on the mattress beside him. Returned from her pre-dawn rambling, she now whispers to herself just as his mother whispered when she thought she was alone. Women's lips moving silently in the dark: there must be some meaning in this: a feminine urge to communicate even when no one is listening?

"Are you all right?" he asks.

She pats his arm. "Yes, Daniel," she says, "I'm fine." Soon she is asleep.

What follows for him is sleeplessness. He skims through twenty-five years, a tape on fast forward—Caro laughing over his stupid jokes, comforting him after his mother's sudden death, her head on the pillow next to him each night, next to him each night through twenty-four years of marriage. He is holding her after the first miscarriage, he is holding her after the second miscarriage, he is stroking her hair and reassuring her they will have two children someday. He has seen it in a dream, a daughter and a son.

§

She traces in her sleep each knot of his spine, each disk connected but separate. When she reaches the base, she runs the tips of her fingers along the bony ridge of his hip. He responds to her touch, buries his head in her skin. She feels the heat of his tongue everywhere at once.

§

She had once been free with her love. She had once danced for him in the lavish white nightgown her mother had given her for the wedding night. The dance made up for the first six days in Monterey, she said, when the closest they had come to intimacy was her throwing up in a trashcan. It was the gown he most remembered, the sheer gown and her body floating toward him. In the lamplight, the gown was her twin, her double, a ghost.

"If I spin fast enough," she says, "I'll rise above the earth."

She twirls in place, once, twice, and then glides across the floor and back on her toes, the rapid, tiny movements of her feet almost imperceptible. She bends to kiss him and, before he can pull her down, leaps away, airborne on the strength of her long, slender legs. Her eyes spot an imaginary point on the wall above the bed as she pirouettes toward him, her head and her raised leg whipping sharply around at the close of every revolution, following the movement of her torso, and her supple arms rise and fall as if they are liquid and the gown floats away from her body and she returns to him, one-two-three-one-two-three, and collapses onto the bed, her arms flailed out, her eyes closed, feigning death.

"I've got just the thing to revive you," he says.

He has relived that night again and again in half-wake or half-sleep. After the children, there were nights of turning away. One night, he woke to her moaning, one hand on her breast, the other in the cleft between her thighs. He wanted her but did not take her, only watched through half-closed eyes, touching himself. He sees her as she was that night, pleasuring herself in a way he never could.

"Let her go," he whispers. "Let her go."

§

She had danced, she had danced, for Dietrich, for Daniel, and the dance could not be undone. Nothing returns to its source. The dream of the white nightgown offers only perfidious protections while Daniel sleeps, he sleeps, and she cannot sleep. Bones lay down to rest and find there is no rest. Coyotes leave, and when they return, they discover there is no return. Hotchkiss roar and buck, a thousand shards of iron cut through shirt and braid, flay flesh and splinter bone. Bullets stray from muzzles, propelled outward until slowed by the friction of their own skin or something soft to spend themselves in, and when they spend themselves, dancers discover they are merely blood and earth. Ghost shirt and nightgown and earth, they are all a gossamer shawl through which she can clearly discern only the shapes of things.

§

He remembers a recurring dream from years ago. In that dream he removed Caro's hand from her breast and bit her there until she cried out. Beneath him she shattered outward from the perfect red oval left by his teeth, like a windshield splintering from a pinpoint of impaled stone. In that dream he left her in pieces.

So easy to bruise a woman, he thinks. She's powerless under you, her body so fragile it feels as if it might break. The dream returns now, unbidden, a waking dream. He takes her hands, the one on her breast and the one on her sex, and pins them to the mattress. Her mouth opens in surprise, and he bites her before she can say no, stop, don't. She cleaves in two, ripping along the seam he has opened in her body, tearing again and again, each fissure doubling and redoubling. He watches her open up to him. Why did he want this? What has he done? This time, he does not leave her broken. He closes each fissure with his tongue, covers her body with his lips until she is whole. It takes a long time and it takes an instant, and all the while, her mouth does not lose its O of surprise, nor does she speak, not when she shatters, not when he heals her.

§

She says nothing because she has vanished under the touch of his lips.

§

At 8:00, he rises to shower, hoping the cold water will do for him what sleep could not. He steadies himself by pressing his forehead against the cool tile, reminding himself that it is Sunday, the day for church service and late breakfast and reading thick newspapers over steaming cups of coffee.

"Sunday," he says aloud, so that this day, devoid of its routine, will not blur into yesterday or tomorrow.

In the bedroom he rifles through his top drawer for a clean undershirt and boxers. He is down to the undershirts with tiny holes ringing the collars, the ones Caro often stole to use for rags. Disreputable, she called them. Who's looking at my underwear? he'd reply. He likes his worn tee-shirts. They are comfortable, broken-in, shaped to fit his torso. He pulls one over his head and glances over at his sleeping wife. She seems for now untroubled by her dreams. The blanket has slipped from her shoulders, and he pulls it to cover her. A miracle they are still together, a miracle she will never leave him. He bends to kiss her forehead, tastes the familiar, salt of her brow.

She opens her eyes and tugs on his undershirt. "Come to bed."

He has never quite gotten over the feel of her skin.

20

From the low outcropping in the rock that serves as its den, the coyote pack fans out across the early spring prairie to forage meat for the fledgling pups. Alone with the father coyote, Caro smells carrion, first flesh, then blood, then marrow. Near the eddy of the creek where Mother Magpie played as a child, in the shade of the dense branching of a weeping willow, on a bed of woven wheatgrass and moistened clay, she sees the bodies—a mother and child offered up by a snowdrift that melts around them. At their feet, creek waters gasp under tender ice floes, which teethe on the frozen mudbanks and break into small sheathes that dance and drift on the whims of the reviving current. Caro pauses to pray over the bodies, almost perfectly preserved by the cold in a posture of protection.

But what the coyote sees is meat and bone, blood and liver and heart, the soft tissue of the brain. He prefers this easy mark to killing because predation consumes energy. One body shielding another means only one thing to him: more food for the pups, his mate, their helpers.

The coyote noses the bodies. They do not strike back. Less timid, he noses the flesh again. They do not strike back. He rips the smaller body from the larger one...no death...tears away the woman's legs from her pelvis with his powerful jaws...no death song...consumes the flesh to carry back in his stomach to the pups...no death song rises...burrows a small hole in the soft earth to cache the bones. No death song rises across the valley.

Flies, roused by the smell of blood, hover, alight on the exposed flesh.

When he is finished, he buries all but the mother's two femurs, grips them in his mouth, and carries them the short distance to the sheltered outcropping where his mate and their four pups wait.

Caro follows him, the coyote unaware of her presence. He drops the long-bones near the bed of grass and fur, regurgitates the flesh to feed the newly weaning pups. With his teeth, he rips the bones into large pieces and offers one to his mate. Then he howls, calling the rest of the pack home.

Soon the pack scavenges among the remains by the nameless creek, near the eddy where Caro first found the bones. Two of the younger males fight over the child's arm bone; one nips at the fingers, one tears at the head. A shard of the thumb bone drops to the earth near the mother's pelvic bone and a piece of the child's skull; the three bones are ground into the mud by the scuffling of coyote feet. The animals are sated, ready to play, and three bones more or less make no difference to them.

21

Leaving Caro to sleep, Daniel wanders down the hall to the kitchen. He is surprisingly, ravenously hungry. Did those few minutes of kissing this morning work up his appetite? He laughs to himself. The warmth of her breath, the sharp corner of her nose against his neck, the vibration of her voice through his skin—all were unexpected.

"A stay of execution," she told him. Maybe the nurse had been right, and all Caro needed was to increase the dosage on her morphine pump.

"Besides," she said, "I felt like kissing you."

They held each other afterward, not talking, though in half-sleep, she spoke to someone in foreign words foreign to him. Not the French she spoke fluently, but something else, repeated and repeated. Hand me—stone? Hand me down? Send in the clowns? He would have to ask her when she woke up.

He opens the refrigerator, hoping to find that a genie has stocked it during the night. If he had three wishes, would he waste one on groceries? Probably. On the shelves are three brown eggs, a carton of orange juice, a cupful of milk in a gallon jug, a scarred apple, some molding cheddar. The thought of shopping—making the list, negotiating the acres of aisles at the local Super Fresh, small-talking with the chirpy Malaysian cashier ("How's your wife?" and then "Have a nice day, Mr. Singleman!")—No.

He throws the cheese in the garbage, which is filled to overflowing (would it kill the kids to take out the trash even once?) and ties the plastic handles together. Outside for the first time in two days, he discovers that spring has arrived. The early April wind is warm against his face, its undertones of bitterness gone. Carried on the breeze is the scent of damp earth and fresh evergreen, of budding trees and root mulch and new leaves of grass. His lawn is covered with a carpet of purple crocuses, the ones Caro and he had planted when they first moved into the house, and birds, hundreds of birds, chatter in unison.

Tossing the garbage bag into one of the rusting metal cans Daniel favors over the giant blue waste containers that have taken over the neighborhood, he bangs down the lid and listens to the clang die away. Disturbed by the noise, the next-door neighbor Richardson's English bulldog—the yapping brute who used to terrify Henry with his demented ferocity—howls. He imagines the dog's crumpled face bunched around a single yawning O. Richardson's wife yells, "Shut up, Boxer!" (an *original* name, he thinks) and her voice carries through an open bedroom window. When Boxer quiets, Daniel bangs the lid again, and the dog howls, and the wife says, "If you don't—" and her husband cuts her off with, "Yes, yes, I'm on it, dear," and farther down the block another dog barks, and then another, and soon the mutts and half-breeds and purebreds of the neighborhood take up the call to arms on the quiet gray and yellow street. Daniel smiles, dusts off his hands.

Back in the kitchen, he punches the coffeemaker's "on" button and pours what is left of the Life cereal and the milk into a bowl. He writes "milk" and "cereal" on a pad by the phone, and then EVERYTHING ELSE underneath. So much for the shopping list.

Just the odor of coffee restores him, and he wonders if the scent might drift down the hall to the bedroom and revive Caro's appetite. It has been months since she could drink coffee, but she used to love the smell, the whole ritual of preparation— grinding the beans, measuring spring water to fill the tank, waiting patiently for the pot to brew. They all knew not to talk to her before that first cup.

He pours himself some coffee, carries his breakfast into the family room, and sinks down into the worn seat cushions of Caro's favorite chair. Bathed in sunlight, he wonders if he will take up where she left off, wandering the house in the early morning hours, a forgetful old man in a faded terry bathrobe and scuffed leather house shoes filling in pages of a journal. Will he be like the transplant patient who acquires the donor's urges—a craving for sushi or the yearning to wind-surf—by taking possession of his wife's habits when she dies? A foolish idea, possession. As if you could stake claim to someone else. Even after all these years, how much does he really know about her? How long will he remember what he does know—the architecture of her bone, the silk of her skin, the taste of her hair?

I'll forget, and then she'll truly be gone.

He spoons some soggy cereal into his mouth, the milk just this side of sour. Sighing, he places the bowl on the side table next to his coffee. The dusty surface is crowded with objects: a small pile of books (always books) and magazines, two engraved silver cups that Alex and Henry had teethed on when they were toddlers, an old to-do list of his with half the items crossed out, and two silver-framed photographs that bracket Caro's life as a mother. One picture is of Caro holding Alex for the first time, his young wife exhausted but content, gazing at her newborn daughter. The other is of Henry in his high school lacrosse uniform, lifting his mother in the air after last year's championship game. His team had won on a fluke goal he had scored in the final seconds to break a 7-7 tie. Improbable moments of grace: his goal, and last May's wind blowing Caro's newly regrown hair away from her face. Her eyes are closed, her head thrown back. It is the very month they discovered the cancer had returned, metastasized to her bones and lymph nodes.

He holds the two pictures side by side. The room is a sea of artifacts just like these, whose meaning, Caro had once told him, could be inferred through association.

"But when we're gone," he responded, "the objects become merely objects again."

"You're wrong," she said. "It's amazing what you can tell from simple markings, the position of one object in relation to another. And then there is the commonality of human endeavor."

The commonality of human endeavor. As if that explained everything. But who will remember the significance of these two photographs except me? Who *will* know that this carved pewter spoon I use to stir my coffee (my life measured out in coffee spoons, isn't that a line from Eliot?) is the same one Henry learned to eat with, or that this silver cup is the one Alex had dented with her new teeth as she weaned from Caro's breast? An archaeologist millennia hence would unearth these objects. A civilized culture, he might say, making art of necessities. Then he would label them and store them in the rummage of wooden drawers.

And what of Caro's breast? A disembodied object like the rest, buried somewhere, or incinerated, and yet, he could still feel it sometimes, cupped beneath his hand, warmth on a cold night, the weight of palmed flesh. He closes his eyes. Those things were no longer real, were they?

He replaces the photos and picks up his coffee, blows across the surface and takes a sip. The black brew (I must remember to get milk) scalds his tongue. He gives up on the coffee, rises from the chair, and crosses to the shelves where Caro keeps her old college books. Running his fingers along the spines, he pulls one old textbook and examines the faded-purple dust jacket.

"*Testimony of the Spade*," he reads aloud. On the cover is a sketch of a golden dragon, a green man wielding a butchering knife over a prone yellow body, a hatchet, an urn, an ancient brooch. A strange mix of myth and matter.

Next to the textbooks are marble copybooks, two dozen black tape spines faded to a mottled gray and arranged in chronological sequence. He removes the first one, unsurprised that she had carefully labeled the cover in block letters:

CAROLINE ANNE PRENDERGAST
FALL 1976
101: INTRODUCTION TO ANTHROPOLOGY

On the opening page are her notes from the first day of class: "Anthropology is the study of human beings in all of their aspects, cultural and physical, through time and space." In the margin, she had written in bold letters: HOW PRESUMPTUOUS! And so it must have gone, through the fall of that year, Caro taking notes in this little book while the leaves changed from green to gold to nothing and the grass browned as the sun angled lower on the horizon and the students hurried across Merion Green to Thomas Great Hall for nine o'clock coffee and donuts. Three decades had passed since she had written these notes, three decades during which the same trees changed colors, the same grass died and regenerated, the same coffee grew cold at coffee hour while undergraduates cornered their professors to clarify points from early-morning lectures.

He replaces the notebook and slips out the next, Introduction to Geology. "Geology shows the world was once a single place," she had written, and then she drew a sketch of Pangaea breaking along crustal plates with copious blue tears coming from the fissures. She is nineteen, sitting in the back of the science lecture hall, her long brown hair pulled up in a sloppy ponytail, sleepily doodling in the margins of the notebook on the first day of classes. She had hated geology.

One after the other, the notebooks reveal the history of her academic life at Bryn Mawr. He comes to the last notebook, Archaeology, a course she had taken in her junior year. An error that it is filed here, he thinks, out of sequence, last in line on the shelf. The notebook itself is unusual, a chaos of sprawling cursive, hasty sketches, and scribbled marginal notes. It looks as if her hand could not keep pace with the lectures.

And it was this course, she had told him, that made her see *things* in a different way. *Things* could be gathered to construct life histories, *things* could narrate the sequent story of the past. It did not matter to her that history would have to change to accommodate each new story.

Over the years they had argued about this very point. It began in their last weeks at school, with a heated discussion of Hesse's *The Glass Bead Game*, which Daniel was reading in his final semester at Haverford. His English professor had tried valiantly to defend the conundrum of history posed by the novel: to retain faith in finding order and meaning in the chaos of conflicting truths while recognizing in advance that one is attempting something fundamentally impossible. Daniel wondered why people put their faith in history, since it was colored by who told the story, whom the storyteller was addressing, and how both understood not only how past events affected the present, but what that present was. Caro had countered that his attitude was defeatist: one had to start somewhere, gather evidence, and build on that knowledge.

"It's possible to know a few things definitively," she said, "and the rest we piece together as physical evidence accumulates. Take Clovis First. Archaeologists developed a story about the first

Americans based on unearthing and dating the Clovis spear point."

"The infamous Paleo-American stroll across the Bering Strait."

"I'm serious."

"I know." He kissed her.

"Did I tell you that evidence from a site in Chile contradicts that theory? That people might have been in the Americas a thousand years before Clovis?" Her voice rises as she continues. "They found a perfectly preserved child's footprint. And a culture, Monte Verde, very different from Clovis."

"So?"

"So, each new story helps us piece together a logical progression of the past. Who knows? There might be something older than Monte Verde. These finds don't erase Clovis, only cast it in a different light."

"But it all depends on who's interpreting the data."

"The evidence doesn't lie. What happens is that those who spent their lifetimes believing that Clovis was first close their minds to other alternatives."

"It's human nature to cling to something that threatens your life's work."

"Human nature, yes, but it's not very scientific!"

He can still see her face, inflamed by the passion of the argument. In the end, weren't we both right? He takes a long, deep breath. We were young once, and fearless.

He flips through the archaeology notebook, its faint blue lines obliterated by notes and drawings illustrating the minutest differences between prehistoric lanceolates, methods and examples of pressure flaking, site grids and soil maps, and even a primitive whistle. In the very center of the notebook is a fine rendering of the human skeleton, so rich in contour and shading that the bones seem alive. Beside the skull is a sketch of a man's head with a face so profoundly lined it appears scarred, and lips so thin they are a gash that divides his crooked nose from his pointed chin. The eyes are two ovals of white narrowing to dark spots, and above each eye, a shadowed cleft echoes the black irises. Was this fanciful projection of the skeleton-man's face a reflection of Caro's need to imbue even some forgotten bones that hung in the corner of the drafty lecture hall with skin, hair, expression, and more—the hints of a story?

In the center divide there is also a loose sheet of paper, folded in half, which he recognizes immediately: his sketch of the glass cathedral, the one he had searched for years before and thought was lost. He examines the drawing in the bright morning light, his fantasy church inspired by Taut's own glass cathedrals. Daniel's model was the mausoleum of the Taj Mahal at Agra, the tomb built by Shah Jehan for his wife. So Caro had tucked this one away for herself? She had good taste for a thief. In the complicated rendering of minarets and domes, he had even accounted for the effect of late afternoon, early winter light.

Fearless, I was, and not that long ago. Was it fear that made me give up these glass monuments for red houses? No, not fear. Was it just the way life goes...on and on...before you can stop it? After all, even Taut abandoned glass for brightly painted houses. Paint was cheap, a way of creating a dwelling at once distinctive and available to everyone.

Daniel traces each crystalline line of the cathedral's central dome. This *is* possible, he thinks. But who is he fooling? The architect who would build the architectures of the future would work for one of the great international firms, and what were his chances of doing that?

He files the sketch safely back in the center divide. He would know where to find it, and Caro would never know he had discovered she had lied to him the day he had searched for the missing cathedral. He flips through the rest of the notebook, page after page of meticulous notes, and the name Dietrich doodled over and over in the margins. On the last page, the very last page, is the same skeleton-man with his cavernous eyes and the gravely lined face.

Dietrich, he says to himself. Of course. The name she has called in her sleep. The professor with the nose hair. His name was Dietrich.

22

Long ropes of Christmas greens drape from the ceiling and festoon the altar, where a tattered banner proclaims PEACE ON EARTH, GOOD WILL TO MEN. The scent of pine comes to Caro first, and then the joy of Christmas morning, so many Christmas mornings bleeding into a single moment of anticipation until she notices the musk of unwashed bodies, the faintly metallic odor of fresh blood. From the organ, "Silent Night," each note separate but muted by other sounds. Coughing, sighing, moaning. The organist's wooden bench is empty, and still the notes rise through the dimly lit mission church. The pews are gone. In their place: rows of bodies, the dying, the just dead.

Three dark-suited doctors walk among the bodies, and still the notes rise singly through the darkness. A fourth man, clad in faded blue jeans and a white shirt, hobbles through the aisle between the bodies with the aid of a walking stick. It is Dietrich. Even more bow-legged than she remembers, he favors his right leg, his odd gait making it appear as if he is walking uphill then down with each step. His hair is completely white, his irises completely black. She can see through his face.

Soiled blue woolen blankets cover the bodies of the dead. Beneath one, something moves. Dietrich limps toward the blanket and Caro follows, afraid of being alone in this church of death. She knows this place, though she has never been here before. It was in the archives she read long ago, the Holy Cross Episcopal Church turned into a hospital, a morgue, after Wounded Knee. The smell nauseates her. Where is the pan Daniel keeps by the bed? Where is the bed?

—Dietrich? she says, and hugs his arm to her torso.

He lifts the corner of the blanket with his walking stick. In the silence single notes sing and a baby girl sucks her dead mother's breast and the flayed tent flap beats in a dying wind somewhere so far away she cannot remember time.

She presses her body closer to him and whispers, —Who speaks for them?

23

Dietrich, Dietrich, Dietrich. He's everywhere in these notebook pages. His words, his image, a curlicue heart pleated with initials doodled in one margin. Was this the same Dietrich she'd dismissed as ancient that afternoon at the airport before she left for South Dakota? Daniel wonders.

How long had the notebooks sat on these shelves, gathering dust in the crevices of their little secrets? *Imagine you could have seen that side of me at the beginning, when we walked for hours along the shore.* Is that why she wants me to recite that damned poem over and over? Imagine knowing anyone in the beginning as you know them later. Why was she insisting on posing a riddle with no solution? Why now?

So what if she had a crush on a college professor a quarter century ago? How did that change what happened between Caro and him? The marriage was real.

He hears her voice again, comforting him over the phone from her parents' home just after he had heard the news that his Vietnam Memorial proposal had been eliminated.

"The design is brilliant," she said. "Just ahead of its time."

It was the very week she had come back from South Dakota. The Lord taketh, and the Lord giveth. Caro had returned. But why had she never spoken of what drove her back a month early? What happened to her in the Badlands, with those bones and that ancient man?

Ancient, he laughs. Dietrich was probably no older than I am now.

Maybe Caro was right after all. The story does change according to its context. Did she realize that even as the books fell? What if those books had stayed on their dusty shelves in the subterranean depths of Canaday, and she had never come to my rescue?

—Are you all right?

She holds her hand out to him. He is too stunned to take it.

Without waiting for a reply, she bends to help him sort and re-shelve the books by their Dewey Decimal call numbers. In three months, she will leave for South Dakota as an assistant on an archaeological dig, and he will leave for Yale and a master's in architecture. They have no future, yet they make one, a future now past, a chain of events set in motion by the domino effect of one book falling into another.

—Are you all right?

She holds her hand out to him.

He takes it. It's warm. She's beautiful.

Caroline! He checks his watch, only to discover a long hour has passed since he left her to have breakfast. Too long. He replaces the notebook exactly where he found it at the end of the shelf, leaving no trace that his wife's filing has been disturbed. At the threshold between the family room and kitchen, he pauses. Why rush? He returns to the notebook (he does not know why) and opens to the glass cathedral and the sketch of Dietrich. He lingers over the two drawings, comparing them side by side. He does not want to think about Dietrich. What of Dietrich? They both had dreams. He folds the drawing of the cathedral in quarters and slips it into his pocket. Clapping the notebook shut, he inserts it where it should have been filed all along, in the middle of the books from Caro's junior year.

24

In the church of the dead and dying, where the ghosts breathe and the living gasp for air, Dietrich strips the blanket from the dead mother and her nursing child and offers it to Caro. The organ goes suddenly silent.

"You're shivering, Caro." Daniel's voice comes from Dietrich's mouth. "Would you like a blanket?"

—Put it back, she says, holding up her hands as if to ward off a blow. —Please put it back.

"Where are you, Caro?" A blanket falls around her shoulders. "Caro?"

She hears Daniel's voice but sees only Dietrich, mocking her with the blanket.

—Here are your Indians. They're not hard to find.

She takes the blanket from him and tucks it around the two bodies. The baby girl continues to suck, oblivious to the ghosts all around her.

—I was meant to find the Miniconjou woman and her son.

—Bones, dear girl. Unidentifiable bones. The bones of a pioneer mother and son lost in the blizzard of 1887? The bones of a French fur trader's wife and daughter lost on their way to Canada? Many people passed through here.

—But only the Sioux made it their home.

—Prospectors, homesteaders, mercenaries . . . hell, even slaves coming north to freedom. You don't know, and what's more important, you'll never know. What we do know is that we have a mammoth kill site. We've established Clovis. And we have a bone tool that pre-dates Clovis. Surely there's more.

—You think.

—I know. We have no time for fairy tales. Consider this: you could use your precious words to trace the line of human history all the way back to the first Americans. Before Beringia.

—Whose lives are more important?

—Isn't it obvious?

The baby exhales, almost a sigh, her mouth letting go the mother's nipple. She replaces the nipple with her thumb. There is Alexandra, sucking her thumb, dozing with her sleeping mother. A passing impression of a winter afternoon years ago. A year of afternoons drinking in the sight of her first child drinking her in. She cannot believe that Alexandra was once so small, small enough to fit in the crook of her arm.

—We're interested in the time for which nothing is written, Dietrich says. —We understand the massacre at Wounded Knee.

—We do? She points to her drawings in one of the field books from the Badlands dig. Where did the book come from after all this time? Yet here it is, it has never left her side: her careful sketches of the woman's ilium, the frontal bone of the child's skull with its shadows for eyes, and the child's right proximal phalanx, the thumb bone Dietrich mistook for pipe. —There's no story for these three bones.

He reaches for the field book, but she pulls it away from him. —You know full well that we can't work with a handful of disarticulated bones contaminated by post-depositional disturbance.

—You mean coyotes? You mean wind, water, earth?

He shrugs. —Why this madness for a couple of dead Indians? And the paperwork for human burial. Dear girl—

—My name is Caroline.

Alexandra has fallen asleep in the Miniconjou woman's arms, her thumb still in her mouth. If only Dietrich would stop talking, she could watch her daughter for a time. How comforting, the slant of afternoon sunlight through the bedroom window on a winter afternoon. She had almost forgotten.

—Caroline. Be reasonable.

Shut up, she wants to say.

—Shut up, she says.

—Caroline. Dietrich's voice is softer now. —We could dig up the entire earth trying to recover our past. You of all people must understand that. We're scientists. What we know about each moment of the past will always be incomplete, most of it lost forever. But the broad strokes we can discover. Who was first? That's an essential question. The essential question. People came to the Americas in waves of migration that corresponded to the periods of glaciation.

—That's a pretty story.

Alexandra snuggles into the woman's breast. She must be cold, Caro thinks, moving toward her daughter.

Dietrich grabs her arm. —Who was first, Caroline?

—You were, she says, shivering with her daughter.

"Are you cold, Caro?" The weight of another blanket settles on her. Her shivering stops.

—Dietrich, nothing's changed. Archaeologists

will fight for years over who was first. One archaeologist's discovery trumps another's. One won't believe the other, or else accuse the other of carelessness.

—My methods have been impeccable for all the years I've worked this site. People quit because I demanded such rigor.

—Really? she says. —We perceive only what we want to see. And you and I both know man's capacity for lying.

—Ah, yes, the serpent in the garden. Didn't God forbid us to eat from the tree of knowledge?

Dietrich offers her an apple suddenly there in his hand. At once she is ravenous. She takes one bite and then another. —And the moment we eat, we die.

He snatches the apple and bites through the flesh. Then with a flick of his wrist, it disappears. —If knowledge is death, then we're dead. We're all dead.

—You *are* dead, Dietrich.

—I certainly didn't die from knowing too much. A heart attack, wasn't it? He touches his fingers to his chest, through his chest, delicately, as if he still expects to feel pain there. He looks relieved. —The fruit was ripe and plentiful. Would the gods miss a single, succulent apple?

He sweeps his hand, and Alexandra vanishes.

—Alexandra! She reaches out toward a widening emptiness, a great chasm where her infant daughter had lain in the arms of the Miniconjou mother, now an exposed pit of bodies stacked like cordwood. Someone strokes her hand.

"Don't cry, Caro. Alex is fine."

"Daniel? Daniel?"

"I'm here," a voice says. But it is Dietrich, and the mass grave at Wounded Knee has been replaced somehow by the mammoth kill site, an open wound of earth gridded with stakes and string, flagged with dozens of metal-edged round white tags marking each microstratigraphic layer—occupation surfaces, fire and trash pits, geologic samplings.

—Perhaps there was an inland waterway through the center of the Americas that opened to this great sea of Kansas, Dietrich says, half to himself. —If we found the remains of a butchered animal, tools beneath Clovis—

—That's your fantasy. Suppose they came in boats, those first Americans. What if they braved the ice-choked Atlantic? Landed in the Carolinas or Virginia?

—A boat of animal hides and wood? It would have been dashed to pieces on the ice during the trans-Atlantic crossing. And where are the boats? Where are the woodworking tools to make the boats? Where are the caves those Solutreans were so fond of painting? The beads with which their women decorated their bodies? The bone flutes on which they played their primitive songs?

—You *have* been gone a long time. Maybe man evolved from the sea itself, from the very salt in the sea? Ha! Maybe even from your precious sea serpents?

Before her, Dietrich's face changes into that of a monosaur, his nose elongating into a snout, his tongue splitting into two halves. She covers her mouth with her hand, stifling the scream that rises there, and then just as suddenly, it is Dietrich's face again before her. The breath has left her body. She bends, gulping fresh air. Someone is kneading the top of her spine.

She straightens up and looks Dietrich in the eye.
—No one knows the truth.

She waves her own hand over the mammoth kill site, and the dead bodies stacked like cordwood again line the open grave. The bodies are clad in white shirts with black birds painted on them. But this could not be. The Seventh Cavalry had stripped the ghost dancers of their shirts: she had read it in the archives. What is this dream of lies within truth? She waves her hand again, and before her is only naked earth demarcated with stakes and string and white tags marking hearths and bones.

—This grid, she says quietly, not quite believing her own voice, this grid is our arbitrary imposition of order on chaos. We tell the story of this place by marking off dirt in squares, as if we can create the truth layer by layer. The story it tells is as true as the story of the coyote who carried Indian bones to her litter.

—We each have our fantasy, then.

—Look at my bones! All of them together still. Can they alone describe me? The last scans of my spine and pelvis with those bright white patches where the cancer is eating through: Do those scans tell me anything except that I will die soon? Maybe that's the truest thing. I'll die soon, as you are dead.

—We have footprints of a mastodon, a leafprint of an unknown flora. The deeper we go into the earth, the more of our story becomes known. Isn't that a nobler goal than these three bones? He presses his index finger on the open page of the field book, on Caro's sketch of the mysterious woman's ilium, and leaves a fingerprint, greasy from the animal middens, on the paper. —You have quite an imagination.

—It's my report. It's permanent.

—Surely you know by now that nothing's permanent. He tears the page from the field book, crumples it, and throws it at her feet. —We're searching for the garden, Caroline. Do you want to stay with me or not?

25

"No, no, no."

"I'm here, Caro. Wake up."

A hand on her shoulder. The touch is solid, gentle, but her eyes will not open to it. Where is Dietrich? Pages from the field book fan out in front of her, create a cool breeze on her face, and then disintegrate into dust. She reaches out to catch the dust, touches flesh. Someone is holding her hand. Dietrich?

"Who's there?"

"Your husband. Daniel. Remember me?"

She grasps his hand tightly, squeezes it, presses it to her cheek. Flesh, warm flesh. "It is you. It's you." Her eyes open. Daniel is sitting next to her on the bed, peering intently at her face. "What just happened? Why am I so hot?"

"You were shivering. I kept putting blankets on you. Too many, I guess."

"I was cold." She watches him peel away two blankets from the pile on top of her, fold them neatly, and stack them on the dresser. The walls are in the wrong place, she thinks, and they're the wrong color. She is surrounded by earth. This is the wrong room. "In the dream," she whispers, touching her throat to feel the vibration there, testing that the voice is hers, "it was winter." Next to the blankets is a bird's nest. A bird's nest? "I was in South Dakota," she says, her fingers still pressed to her throat, her voice a little stronger, "and it was cold." It is her voice, yes, but next to the bird's nest, a disembodied head, her disembodied head, her hair and a faceless head. "I was frightened." Her voice catches.

"Are you OK?" The words come, not from Daniel, but from a shadow on the far wall, and from the dream she can see the translucent form of Dietrich, so old he was, older than she thought he could be. She trembles involuntarily, and then winces from the sudden pain the spasm causes at the base of her spine.

"You're not OK, are you? On a scale of one to ten…"

"Spare me." She blinks slowly. When she opens her eyes, the wall is just a long expanse of pale terracotta, the head is the Styrofoam form that holds the wig she had rarely worn, the bird's nest is her mother's hairbrush tangled with her own long brown hair, and the shadow is only her husband's shadow cast by the morning light coming through the picture window.

"You know how much I hated that damned questionnaire," she says. "Every day the same questions. 'Do you have pain when you're sitting still?' Check. 'Do you have pain when you're moving around?' Check. 'Have you tried meditation?' Clever. 'Is the pain constant?' Is the Pope Catholic? 'Where is the pain most severe?' Everywhere. 'What feelings increase the pain?' Joy, sorrow, fear. 'How would you describe your pain?' Sharp, shooting, stabbing, steady, searing. Check. Check. Check. Check. Check."

"It would've been a bestseller—*Caro's Diary of Pain*."

"Don't...make...me...laugh." The laughter causes a sudden stabbing pain in her lung, and she breathes in sharply.

"When was the last time you took the morphine?"

"I'm full up." She points to the pump as if to prove her point.

He picks up the box of morphine injectors. "What about these?"

"It's better now, better," she says, forcing a tight smile. "Where are the kids?"

"The kids? Last I saw them they were on the roof."

"Have you lost your mind?"

"We were having a howling contest," he says. "I lost."

"*You* were on the roof?"

"They're fine. Still sleeping. We were up late talking, and then they let me tuck them in." He touches his finger to her nose. "So why were you dreaming about South Dakota?"

"I was in a church. A cold church where they housed the injured after Wounded Knee. I read about that place. In the archives where records—"

"Why did you come back early?"

"I was a shovel bum, that's all, the lowliest of God's creatures, and it's a long story."

"We have time."

"Time rushes past, and we see nothing but sand," she says. "Angels visit us, but we only know them when they're gone." She sighs. "Bone flutes and sea serpents and dead Indians. Make your mind hold each one when they're stacked like so much wood."

"Are you sure you're all right?" He touches her forehead. "Maybe you have a fever? Or need something to eat?"

"Food burns my throat." She presses his hand to her cheek. This is real. She pulls him down to sit beside her. "Do you remember when Alex was an infant, and I spent whole afternoons just lying with her in bed?"

"I remember coming home from work

and finding you right where I left you in the morning."

"To think I'd almost forgotten those days."

Still holding his hand, she looks through the wide pane of glass that frames the front yard. The anorexic sycamore is just beginning to leaf and shade the winter-burned lawn, and the quiet of winter mornings has given way to the murmuring of swallows and the nattering of jays, who perch on the neat row of bricks that line the outside sill. In the distance the calling of crows reminds her that this is the season of her death, the spring she loves so well. It is as good a time as any to reveal the truth.

"Do you really want to know why I returned?"

"Yes."

She turns back to him. "The truth is I left for the children's sake. For the children, and you."

"But we weren't even married yet."

"Nearly so." She studies his face, wondering if she can read his mind. The skin around his eyes is puffy from lack of sleep, but his eyes are the eyes of the Daniel she knew when he was twenty-two. He will forgive her. "You remember Dietrich?"

"That ancient professor of archaeology?"

"He was fifty then. You're almost fifty." She runs her fingers along his cheekbones. Yes, the same eyes. *You're the first, Caro*, he confessed to her when they finished making love, after her spectral dance. Then he ran his tongue through her hair. She had almost forgotten that, the feeling of his wet tongue pressed against her scalp. She had placed her hands on his ears and turned his face to hers. The first, she said to him, and kissed him on each cheek.

"So you're jealous of a dead man?"

"He died?"

She nods. "He was a difficult man. We fought. We fought all the time."

"That's good." He laughs, and she pretends to slap his hand.

She can read his mind. She knows what he thinks he will hear, what he does not want to hear. *I slept with him in the tent of bones.*

"Remember those bones I found? He made me leave them in one of the drawers, mislabeled as bison bones."

In the pile of bones, Sioux garbage.

"I wanted to bury them again. I had this vision of myself, sneaking into the workroom late at night, stealing the bones. You know, the archaeologist in the white hat. But . . . "

I was young, Daniel.

"I meant to bury them. Isn't that the same thing? Dietrich stayed on for years in that bitter place."

I meant nothing to him.

"I guess I didn't want what he wanted, or didn't want it enough, or I wanted this more."

I betrayed you.

"In the end I felt I couldn't betray him, or he had some strange power over me. He knew what he wanted. But those three bones—"

"I'm confused. Aren't you talking about the Miniconjou mother and her son? I thought you buried them."

"That's what I told you then. But what I told you wasn't exactly the truth." *Forgive me.* It would be so easy to tell him now. "The truth is, there was no way to prove whose bones those were. I had the osteologist run tests. He said the salts and minerals proved the bones to be contemporaneous, one hundred years old, give or take. We knew that the pelvis was a young woman who had had a child. The other bones were those of a child of indeterminate age, probably less than twelve." This is true, all true. "That's all we knew. That and they were together, the only human bones we ever found at the site."

She looks over at the faceless head wearing the wig she never got used to wearing. For an instant, she sees Mother Magpie's face in the blank white stare. And then it is just her own face she sees. "Whoever they were, they deserved a decent burial. I didn't give it to them. If I had stayed . . . I couldn't stay." Tears are burning her throat, tears enough, she thinks, to dissolve the sky. "Forgive me, Daniel."

"There's nothing to forgive." Daniel hugs her to him. "I'm sure you did what you could. You did enough."

"Enough?" she says. "What I did was nothing." She presses her hand against his chest, pushes him away, and turns from him. "Leave me alone."

26

Caro watches the bedroom door close behind Daniel. He is, she thinks, just beginning to learn her capacity for cruelty. Come back, come back, come back. But the door remains closed, and then it disappears, and then the walls bend and twist inward to envelop her in their earth. Help me. Everything goes black for a moment, and the walls exhale. Yes, the walls are breathing. There is a sudden loosening in her chest, as if something has torn itself free inside her, but it does not hurt.

Every object in the room defies gravity, floats free, moves with the room's breathing. The Styrofoam head drifts over to the slip chair, hovering above the gold upholstery, and a pale form wavers beneath.

—Hello, Mother, Caro says. —Is there something you've forgotten?

—Just one thing.

As Mother settles in the bedroom chair, the objects in the room settle too. Everything is still and silent. The room has ceased to breathe.

Mother adjusts the folds of her white robe, and her heart glows red beneath the diaphanous garment. —In the beginning, she says, was the earth. Good lands made bad by man's desires.

—Was it only man's desires that shaped the land?

Mother shakes her head. —Moisture, when it freezes, has the power to split rock. Fire, when it burns, reshapes the prairie. Even grass roots, seeking life in the vein cut by decaying leaves, over time cut swaths through the Stronghold's cliff face.

—And what of your dreams?

—They weather the earth.

27

"Who's there?" Caro asks. "Mother?"

But this vision is not a heart and a voice robed in white. It is a man, but not quite a man, something is off, something not right. A ghost in boxers and a sleeveless undershirt? spiky brown hair shaped into cresting waves, waves of a dark ocean? a chin shadowed with shadow? "Little Magpie?"

"Where's Dad?" The vision persists. It wants information.

"Dad? He's dead," she says. "He died long ago."

"He can't be dead," the young man says, shuffling over to her bedside, touching her shoulders. "Stop it, Mom. Mom?"

The face shapes itself into familiar outlines, the deep cleft of the chin, the hard, high cheekbones, the eyes bathed in liquid brown swimming toward her. Henry looms over her, silently studying her face. At six-two, he is only an inch shorter than his father, his shoulders broad and his stomach lean from weight-lifting at the high school gym. He had been building up for the new lacrosse season, but the season started without him. She urged him to go out for the team, but he just shrugged. He would stay with her, that silent shrug said.

"Where's Dad?"

"He's probably gone to fix me one of those awful milkshakes he knows I won't drink." She pats the empty space beside her. "You look tired."

He does not move. "I'm OK."

"Come on." She pats the bed again. "Keep me company."

He sits gingerly on the edge of the bed as if the slightest movement of the mattress will break her. He had been home alone with her the afternoon the pain in her spine became so much like flame she thought she would literally burn alive. She remembers screaming, the sound emanating not just from her mouth, but from her whole body, as if every pore had found a voice, and Henry shouting into the phone, C'mon, c'mon, my mother is dying here, hitting his thigh with his open palm, too nervous even to bite his fingernails, and the EMTs busy with their needles and oxygen masks, and then oblivion. That was the day they started the morphine.

"I didn't sleep last night," he says finally.

"That makes us a family of insomniacs. Maybe your father decided a hit of coffee was in order. Isn't that coffee I smell?" She picks up an empty syringe from the nightstand and waves it in front of him. "Maybe he can just inject it in our veins."

"That's not funny, Mom." He grabs the syringe and throws it on the nightstand.

"It *is* funny, actually." She turns toward him and strokes the small of his back, something that used to soothe him as a child. "Remember that day you ran screaming from the pediatrician's office with the needle sticking out of your arm?" It was a test for tuberculosis, and the needle had to be left in the arm until a lump was raised. Now count to ten! the nurse had chirped, and he sat in Caro's lap obediently counting to ten, his eyes squeezed shut, and then all of a sudden he leapt from her grasp and ran away. "I've never seen you so angry."

"The nurse lied."

"Yes, she lied. Would you have let her put the needle in if you had known the test lasted thirty seconds?"

"I didn't have TB." He glares at her, six years old and standing by the elevator, rubbing the spot on his arm where the needle had been. You hurt me, he had said. And then he punched the down button and refused to talk to her on the ride home.

"C'mon, honey." She tugs at his arm. "Let's talk about something else."

He stretches out next to her, in his father's familiar space, his body warming hers. Someday, she thinks, he'll lie next to his wife like this. In five years or ten? He'll be someone's husband, father to her grandchildren. "And I won't even know their names."

"Whose names?" he asks.

"It's not important. Look at me."

He turns to her, his face so close she can count the pores on his nose. He averts her gaze and begins to worry a hangnail.

"You know, that habit had its good points." She takes his hand from his mouth and kisses it. "I don't think I ever had to cut your nails. Saved me scads of time." She twines his fingers in hers, thinking she could simply walk out of this life with him, let the earth cover them. After she died, would she be able to touch him like this?

"Your fingers, my pelvis, Alex's skull," she whispers. "The bones find each other. They last and last. They outlive time." She is in the limitless sea, digging and digging, laying the bones gently one on top of the other. "You see, we'll be together. Just like them."

"You're scaring me."

"Oh, God, Henry, I'm sorry. It's just the morphine talking." She forces herself to concentrate on her son, the straight plane of his nose, the hair growing from the mole on his right cheek, the way his mouth changes shape as he speaks. "What do you want to talk about?"

He pauses again, looking at her face. "What's it like, Mom? I mean, what do you think about?"

"Anything, everything. Crazy things. A couple of nights back, I kept seeing a kaleidoscope of knives, just that, over and over. Reliving my surgeries, I suppose. Maybe a part of us remembers, even under anesthesia."

He is quiet beside her. She searches for something else to talk about, something that will not scare him. "Like I've been thinking about the first year your father and I were together. Or not together. I was in the Badlands looking for evidence of the first Americans."

"That must've been cool."

"Actually, it was mostly grunt work. Sometimes even a mason's trowel was too blunt a tool for excavation. Imagine removing a layer of dirt with a razor blade. Twelve hours a day, seven days a week. The same corner of rock. And the sun beating—"

"I get the picture."

"OK, then." The knot on the top her spine begins to burn. She reaches for the button on her pump, tells herself *not now,* then presses her fingers into the pain. "The big problem as far as Dietrich was concerned—Dietrich was the supervisor—the big problem was that the topmost layers of the small area to which I was assigned contained Native American artifacts—pieces of clay pipe and remnants of fire pits—and lots of discarded animal bones. He didn't want to be bothered, you know, dealing with all that Indian stuff."

She takes a deep, unhurried breath, the air scraping against her windpipe. The breath of the dying, she thinks. Does Henry notice? She looks at his face, but he is simply watching her, waiting for the rest of the story.

"Not too far from where I worked, in a much deeper trench, Dietrich discovered what appeared to be a bone tool that pre-dated anything anyone had ever uncovered in the Americas. He was obsessed with the belief that there was more, drove us to find other evidence of the unknown culture."

"He sounds like a psycho."

"Megalomaniacal, really. There were others like him who believed that it was a matter of digging deep enough into the earth. And he wanted the glory."

"So, did he ever find what he was looking for?"

She shakes her head. "Archaeologists found at other sites what Dietrich only dreamed of finding." Dietrich appears, briefly, a shadow in the corner of her eye. "Go," she says, waving her hand in a dismissive gesture.

"You want me to leave?"

"Not you, sweetheart." She pulls Henry into her arms as the wall opens then closes around Dietrich's body, swallowing him whole, and she shudders at the sudden recollection of the image from her dream: Alex disappearing into the mass grave at Wounded Knee.

"When I unearthed three human bones—a piece of a woman's pelvis, a tiny thumb bone, and a frontal bone from here," she says, and taps his forehead, "Dietrich was furious. We weren't digging in a known burial ground. And the Sioux believe that graves shouldn't be disturbed. That the soul lingers if the grave is left intact. Of course, these bones had been disturbed by something, probably animals, before I found them. I wanted to bury the bones... just there, over the rise... there, beside the creek... a woman cradles her son, whispers through the falling snow 'everything will be all right,' so he won't cry as he smothers in his own breath and, over a century, water seeps through the sediment, forming a cave of the bodies—"

"Stop it," he says gulping down a sob. "That isn't real."

"I'm sorry, Henry. Those were just lines from a poem I never finished." She hugs him tighter, more fragile than she suspected, his ragged breathing rhyming hers. "Would it help you to know that this doesn't seem real even to me?"

She has not held him like this since he was a small boy. He is living, breathing flesh. She is fading, dissolving, incorporeal. What is real is the pain, which defines her body, its borders. It is everywhere, even in her toes. "I don't know what else I can tell you."

He looks at her, eye to eye, without blinking. "I think if I don't fall asleep, you'll still be here. I think if I look at you hard enough, you can't die. I think, this is my mother, she's here, she's now."

"I *am* here, Henry." She kisses him on the cheek, her lips brushing the stubble on his chin. It is Daniel's face under her lips, as he was earlier this morning—was it just this morning?—holding her lightly and kissing her as if she were still the same woman he loved, the one he once thought was beautiful.

She loosens her hold on Henry, and he relaxes in her arms. "The Sioux tell the story of a beautiful woman two warriors meet while hunting buffalo. She's so beautiful that one of the hunters wants her for his own. His friend warns him that the woman is *wakan*, holy, but the foolish hunter reaches out to touch her anyway. Immediately, a great cloud surrounds him, and when it clears, all that's left is a pile of bones writhing with snakes."

"Is that some kind of lesson for me?" Henry asks.

"Don't be ridiculous," Caro says. "Where was I?"

"Some guy gets eaten by snakes for *almost* touching a woman."

"Exactly." She smiles, ruffles his hair. "So the other hunter is pretty scared. The holy woman tells him not to be afraid, but to return to his people and have them prepare for her arrival by building a tipi in the center of camp. She promises to bring them a great gift. A few days later, the people hear singing, and on the cloud of singing comes this same woman, even more beautiful than the surviving hunter remembers. She's dressed from head to toe in white, and her hair flows behind her like a river of black ink. Her gift is a pipe made of red stone, carved with a buffalo calf and decorated with eagle feathers. 'This pipe,' she says, 'is sacred, and its powers will help you through dark times.'

"Blessing the people, she shows them how to use the pipe to pray. Then, she teaches them how to live. She turns to the men and tells them that they must care for their families, that the pipe binds them to their wives for life. She turns to the women and tells them they're as important as the men, since they bear the children and do the work that keeps everyone alive. She turns to the children and tells them that they're the future of their people. And then she sings, and rising into the song, she turns into a white buffalo calf and vanishes into the setting sun."

"A *white* buffalo?"

"Yes, white. It's rare. The Plains Indians considered it sacred. Of course, the buffalo itself was sacred—"

"I read somewhere that the government knew, you know, that if the buffalo dwindled, the Indians would come to depend more and more on the government. So they encouraged the homesteaders and Chinese railroad workers to hunt down the buffalo for food, or to trash the meat and skins and use the bones for fertilizer. They even let some companies grind the bones for china."

He rambles on, her old Henry, imparting just a trace of his vast knowledge of settlers and wagon trains, the way West and the railroads and the many trails of tears. He is speaking rapidly, his eyes clear and bright. Where had he gone, oh, where had this boy gone, and would he return when she was gone? It might take months, it might take years, it might take forever. No. He would recover, she had to believe that, or she could not leave. Or only part of her could leave. A piece of her—hand, eye, heart—left behind as he is left behind. Her heart just there, beating on the bed.

"Are you listening, Mom?"

"To every single word."

"I'm serious." His face tightens along the jawline, and here is the new Henry, opaque as stone, transparent as glass. "Why did you tell me that story?"

She runs her fingers along his stubbled cheek. "I wanted you to know that... I don't know why. Because the story was part of me and now it's part of you?" She kisses his forehead. "Henry, dear, take one of my rings, or that gold cross I used to wear, something you can hold on to, something—"

"I don't want *things*. I don't want anything from you." He breaks away from her, rises suddenly from the bed. "This sucks, Mom. It sucks, and there's no way to make it better."

She holds her hand out to him, but he is already out of reach. He strides out of the room, not even pausing to look at her. He is gone. Eyes stinging, she balls her fists, squeezing them so tight the nails dig into her palms. Pain pierces each of her vertebrae, as if needles prick the nerves that run along the spinal column. He is right, of course. No way to make any of this better.

Good-bye, Henry, good-bye.

She presses the button on her morphine pump and closes her eyes.

—Oh, there you are. You're here.

28

Henry is running along a cliff that falls away to rocks and an endless chasm. He does not realize the danger he is in. He is an egg, running along the cliff, and if he falls, no one can put him back together. Daniel reaches out, he touches his son, a candlestick crashes into the dining room table.

Lucid dreaming, he laughs to himself, and rights the candlestick. All the King's horses, and all the King's men. Why do we tell that horrible nursery rhyme to our children?

He presses two fingers into his ribcage where Caro elbowed him during the night. She was still capable of hurting him. *Leave me alone.* The ache has worsened, and he cannot inhale deeply without feeling a sharp pain in his ribs.

On a scale of one to ten, how would you rate your pain? A negative ten, you wimp.

A carefully fanned apple sits browning on the plate in front of him. He had thought to bring the fruit to Caro, casually place it on the nightstand. Maybe the apple, its sweet smell or the beauty of red and white against the pale yellow plate, would tempt her. But then he found Henry in bed with Caro, the two of them deep in conversation, and he did not want to disturb them.

He pops one of the slices into his mouth, chews it methodically, and swallows, watching his Adam's apple move down then up in the mirror that dominates one wall of the dining room. There is Caro in the mirror, holding the newly christened Alex—Caro and Alex, a hundred echoes of them, and a single image of him, his face obscured by the camera and the rays of its explosive flash.

The flash momentarily blinds him. Light shines through the X-ray of Caro's spine, and eerie white patches glow where cancer has obliterated bone.

—Here, here, or here, the radiologist says, tapping the X-ray on each of the brightest patches. —Any one of these places, her spine could break. Such a break could result in permanent paralysis, or even instant death.

The doctor turns to Daniel. —Do you understand what I'm saying? We have nothing left to offer you. Her case is medically futile.

—Her case? He smashes his fist on the X-ray, and the glass beneath the transparency shatters but the panel remains intact, a web of vein-like cracks superimposing itself on the image of his wife's skeleton. —Here, here, and here, he says, pointing to the same bright patches. —That's my wife!

He rips the X-ray off the light panel. Pebbles of glass, suddenly unfettered, spill to the floor, and the machine's naked light floods the dark room. He squints through the bright light and finds only the morning sun hitting the dining room mirror. No one is there, not the young doctor, not Caro.

Caro. Despite what she said, she should not be alone. He struggles to sit up, but even the simple act of rising through gravity overwhelms him.

She is an egg, she is falling, he cannot move.

His feet are sinking through the carpet.

Leave me alone. Let Dietrich go to her, then.

His head hits the tabletop, startles him awake. He cannot face her. No matter what the grief therapist tells him, he is weary of pretending the normal things matter. Trash, bills, vomit.

I won't go. I'm not a hero, not one of the King's men. Not even one of his horses.

A horse's head forms in front of him, and beneath it, the body of a woman, and it is, he somehow realizes, Caro's medical team coordinator. The horse-woman is speaking into a black headset. —Why subject her to another surgery? That growth on her navel won't kill her. She huffs twice into the phone, clearing her throat. —You know your wife is dying, don't you?

He rubs his eyes. Except for the piles and piles of paperwork—medical bills, explanations of benefits, denials of claims—the table is empty. No horse's head, no X-ray, no wheezing administrator. But he remembers clearly last week, the coordinator with the mouthful of teeth (a horse's mouth, that's it) raising her voice when he refused to answer her question. He had, instead, held the phone away from him while her voice continued to rise. "Hello, hello, *hello*? Mr. Singleman? Did you hear what I said?"

He was silent as she tapped on the receiver, as if sending a message by Morse code. "Hello?" she said again, and then he banged the phone down on the cradle.

So, they will leave that *thing* growing from her navel. They did not have to clean it every day with a Q-tip and hydrogen peroxide. A leech, he thinks, draining her even as I feed her. It will be there when she dies. And after she dies, it will continue to grow, something alive feeding off her dead body, a skeleton with that *thing* still protruding, still thriving on whatever is left of her.

Let her break, let her break, I'm finished.

He falls back into the chair, and the disturbance in the air causes several of the papers on the table to rise up and waft to the ground. He bends to pick them up, shuffling them into a neat stack. The topmost paper has many numbers neatly circled in red, numbers Daniel remembers marking months ago. They are portions of each procedure, or the procedures themselves, which the insurance company refuses to cover. The reasons are explained in footnotes whose lettering is too small to read, but the gist is that the doctors had not followed the proper sequence of testing before Caro's last round of chemotherapy. The balance owed, which has carried forward from hospital bill to hospital bill, is more than he and Caro borrowed to mortgage their home. If forced to pay, he will have to re-finance the house to cover it. Surely they will not try to collect from a dead woman and her grieving husband. Surely they will.

He places the papers back in the piles he has decided to ignore until after her death. The dust on the tabletop is thick. In it he doodles lines, parallels and perpendiculars, which become squares he connects with more lines, which become cubes within cubes within cubes. His life has been measured out, not in coffee spoons, but lines, infinitely connected lines, straight lines and curved lines, lines that divide and lines that dissolve and lines that diminish to the point of nothing. He polishes away the cubescape with the sleeve of his robe and admires the gleaming mahogany surface.

The dining room set was the first real furniture they had ever purchased—an undocumented Philadelphia Barry Chippendale table and eight matching chairs. Three months' salary, a wild extravagance, and he did not even like antiques. He runs his fingers over the acanthus leaves carved into the curved edge, along the V-shaped passage between the leaves. If the table had been authenticated, it would have cost much more. Had he thought eight elegant ribbon-backs and a delicately carved table might somehow replace their two lost children?

Two lost babies. The first conceived broken. They induced Caro at five months, the little girl arriving whole, almost perfect, with part of her brain missing. He held her until she ceased moving. The baby's image still haunts him. Mercifully, Caro was asleep. The other one's loss was easier to bear—a simple miscarriage at ten weeks' gestation. Sex indeterminate and the heart never formed, the report said. Somewhere in the fifth week, a fire that should have sparked failed to ignite. They saw it on the ultrasound, the space where the heart should have been in a body, the space where the baby should have been in the heart.

And then Caro, kneeling in front of him once again. —I'm pregnant.

She is pregnant. She puts her head in his lap, he strokes her hair, an hour passes. He strokes her hair, her head in his lap, and they say nothing. They keep the news to themselves, they will not tell a soul, not even her mother, who still calls every morning to chat, who still inquires as to when she might become a grandmother. No, they will sit here for nine months and everything will be fine if they simply sit here for nine months.

—I'm pregnant, she says.

The book of Alex, and then the book of Henry, one book falling into the next.

He wakes to discover his head on the seat cushion of the chair beside him. Caro is not there. Maybe she is calling to him and he cannot hear her, or maybe she is having trouble breathing, or maybe even the slight weight of her emaciated body pressing on her spine has broken it. And so she will die in a borrowed bed in a borrowed room while he sits here. Quick, painless, and no one will blame him.

He traces a deep gouge that interrupts the leaf pattern in the table's carved edge, a blemish that marked the table when they purchased it: someone else's child in someone else's dining room, a little boy in knickers chasing his sister in her hoop skirt, wild laughter, a carelessly turned head, a body falling against the chair, the chair falling into the table. And then a vast white space until... the scratches left by Henry's metal soldiers, imaginary battles reenacted over and over on the vast wooden plain. Yorktown, the Alamo, Custer's Last Stand. Alex's accidental cursive etched in the space where she had preferred to do her homework. How he had yelled at her. She ran to her room crying and did not come out for the rest of the day. In that way she was so much like her mother, so much alike in their punishing silences. Punishing him with emptiness, the sound absence makes, like holding one's breath underwater.

Silent on the examining table and draped only with a blue paper gown, Caro twists her gold wedding band around her finger. The doctor listens to her heart.

—A human guinea pig. That's what you're telling us. She'll be a human guinea pig, Daniel says.

The doctor turns to him, his nose elongating into a snout. The change does not surprise Daniel; he has suspected it all along.

—It *is* experimental, the pig-faced doctor says, towering over Caro's half-clothed body.

—And what would it buy us? A month? Two?

—It's her only chance. We can't even guarantee you'll be getting the medicine or the placebo. He scratches his snout with a cloven hoof. —Otherwise—

—Can you at least guarantee she won't suffer?

The pig just shakes his head and retreats to his desk, where he sits shuffling papers and snuffling and shrinking and shrinking until there is nothing but an empty dining room chair, and then Caro is there, sitting silently before him in the same chair, listening to him lay out all the reasons why it is time to stop. He cannot hear the words coming from his own mouth, they sound like nonsense, like nursery rhymes told to children simply to scare them.

—I'll die without it, is all she says to him when he finishes his speech. His head hurts from too much and not enough. Then night, and she is dreaming night, she must be dreaming night and sees what he sees, everything he sees. But what he sees is only what he sees.

And then she is sitting before him again, in the same dining room chair with the morning light filling her lap, and she is telling him that she has spent the night thinking and you're right, it's not worth it, she says.

If he could just reach out and catch the words trapped inside the little bubbles in the air surrounding her head—Humpty Dumpty had a great fall, ashes to ashes, flying pigs and talking horses and cats eating blind mice, and farmer's wives with butcher's knives, and suffer the little children, suffer, break, and die—if he could just catch the words and stuff them back into his mouth—he reaches out and grabs one word—no—

—No, he says, we can take it.

She says nothing. Her hands are folded in her lap, and the sun glints off the gold band on her ring finger. She is fading into the ring's reflected light.

—No, he says again. —I can take it if you can. I can take it.

He wakes, punching the tabletop. "I can take it," he says aloud. His voice echoes in the empty dining room.

"It *is* time to stop," she had said. "Only promise me you'll stay home at the end."

The hospice nurse came two days later. She walked through the front door with a chipper smile and a stethoscope draped around her neck and her white shoes squeaking on the front hall terrazzo. She was kind and gentle and smelled like rubbing alcohol. She made it seem, for an hour each day, as if competence and efficiency could save Caro's life. For an hour each day, someone else could clean the vomit and change the bandages and replace the pads that absorbed the fluid from her weeping legs. And maybe, just maybe, if there was a God, and if that God, that hidden God, were a compassionate God, Caro would die on the nurse's watch. From the book of common prayer he prays, Let me be there when she dies. Don't let me be there when she dies.

He buries his head in the crook of his arm. Just ten minutes of blessed sleep, he thinks, and Henry is an egg running along a cliff falling away to jagged rocks. Alex is an egg, chasing him, and Caro, the largest egg of all, lags behind them. Then they are falling all at once. If he could slow down time, just slow it down a little, he could catch each one separately and guide each gently to earth. There is no earth, only space. They are falling into nothing.

"Dad! Dad!"

"You're not an egg," he says sleepily.

"Wake up, Dad! Mom's calling for you," Alex shouts. "Something's wrong."

29

Daniel and Alex find Caro sprawled facedown in the bed, slapping the mattress with her palms, her mouth open in a scream from which no sound comes. Her nightgown is soaked through, and it clings like wet tissue to her thighs and her back.

"Help...me," she says, the words so choked with phlegm he understands them only by the shapes her lips make.

He sits on the edge of the bed, motioning with his finger for Alex to circle the bed and do the same. Obediently, she responds.

"Grab her hands." They lean toward Caro, and press her hands lightly into the mattress. Her body stills, but her breath quickens, and perspiration breaks out in tiny beads along the crown of her bare scalp. Alex bites her bottom lip, staring at him, stifling the urge to cry. With his free hand, he quickly squeezes his daughter's shoulder and mouths, "Go."

Alex shakes him off. "I'm staying."

No time to argue, he turns to Caro. "You took the morphine?"

"Just...it's not...working." She clasps his hand so hard he feels the bones of his knuckles crack and bunch.

"What about those?" He points to the box of morphine injectors on Alex's side of the bed.

"I can take it." She turns toward him, her eyes pinched so tight tears leak from the corners. The grimace renders her face an eyeless skull, and he thinks briefly of her body in the grave.

"Caro, honey," he says, cupping her shoulder blade through her wet nightgown, "one extra dose won't kill you."

"How the hell do you know?"

"The doctor said—"

"The doctor said, the doctor said. The doctor said I'm supposed to be dead. Do I look dead—oh, oh, oh—"

"Alex, give me one of those."

She releases her mother's hand and removes a plastic vial from the box. Caro slips from Daniel's grasp, flips over, and bats the vial out of Alex's hand. It flies across the room and hits the far wall, skittering to the floor.

"What did I do? What did I just do?" she screams. "I can't move."

"Mom!" Alex says, and grabs her arms.

"Caro!" Daniel says, too sharply. One, two, three, four, he counts silently. "Calm down, sweetheart. Let me see what happened."

"I'm burning," she says through clenched teeth. "Help me!"

Bowing her head, Alex whispers, "Please, God, please, please, please."

"Mom?" Henry is in the doorway, rubbing his eyes.

"Get out!" Daniel says.

"Don't shout at him!" Alex says.

Caro takes a long, jagged breath and exhales as if a metal whistle is lodged in her throat. "I'm dying, I'm dying, this is what it's like to die." She shakes her head back and forth, no, no, no.

Five, six, seven, eight, she can't be paralyzed if she can still move her head, Daniel thinks.

"I'm calling 9-1-1," Henry says, and reaches for the phone.

"No." Daniel grabs his son's arm harder than he means to. "She doesn't want that. That's the last thing she wants." He turns to Alex. "Get another one."

Silently, she removes a second vial from the box, slides the injector from its protective case, and turns it horizontally in the sunlight, squinting at the tiny print of the directions. The brightly-colored plastic cylinder looks innocuous in the morning light, cradled in his daughter's delicate hand, like a child's toy. "Dad?"

"Give it to me, Alex." He holds out his hand; she hesitates before placing the injector in his palm. Trembling, Caro stares at the tube, and then at Daniel.

"Henry, hold Mom's leg still."

Henry takes two steps toward the bed, stops, and shakes his head. "I can't, Dad."

"Dammit, Henry, *now*."

He takes one more step forward, then holds out both hands in front of him. "I can't."

"I'll do it," Alex says. She holds her mother's leg while Daniel tears the foil packaging from an alcohol wipe with his teeth and swabs a spot on the thickest part of Caro's thigh.

"No," Caro moans. "No."

Suddenly Henry leans forward and holds his mother's face gently between his hands. "It'll be okay in a second, Mom. Hang in there. Just hang in there one more second…"

Soothed by his son's rhythmic monotone, Daniel detaches the red safety and jabs the injector firmly against her outer thigh. There is a hiss as the hidden, spring-driven needle releases, and he tightens his grip against the mechanism's unexpected recoil.

30

Daniel, Henry, and Alex sit on the bed in a semi-circle around Caro, watching her as though watching a silent movie. Alex strokes her mother's arm, lightly running her fingers up and down, up and down, as she has for the past fifteen minutes. The used injector lies in Daniel's open palm. He looks at it, almost surprised to see it there. The needle shimmers with tears of liquid morphine, oddly beautiful.

"Is she...?" Henry asks, his voice barely a whisper.

"Sleeping," Daniel says softly, and squeezes his son's arm. "Just sleeping."

He deposits the injector in the orange Sharps container on the nightstand. It drops to the bottom with a hollow tap, tap, tapping.

Then he takes Caro's hand in his own and notices for the first time that her skin is tinged faintly blue. Cyanosis of the extremities. Not a good sign.

"I can stay here," Daniel says. "Why don't you two get some breakfast?"

"I'm not hungry," Henry says.

"Me either," Alex says. "Is she cold? I think she's cold. She's cold." She places her mother's arm under the covers and neatly folds the yellow blanket across her body.

Daniel follows suit, tucking the other arm under the covers. "You two were remarkable."

"I thought the deal was that she died without pain," Alex whispers fiercely. "Wasn't that the deal? The morphine meant no more pain?"

"Doctors lie. Either that, or they just don't know. They never want you to lose hope." He brushes Alex's hair away from her face. "Mom hasn't been using enough of the morphine. You know how she feels about it."

"This is better?" Henry asks.

"Well, it's either this or … " He shrugs, trying to stay calm for their sake, though his throat is burning. What little breakfast he managed to eat is turning to acid in his esophagus. He swallows, and then realizes he has been counting. Twenty, he says to himself, but he does not remember starting at one.

"Would it be okay if I went back to bed?" Henry asks in the wake of the silence. "I mean . . . shit."

"Go on," Daniel says. "We'll call you if anything changes."

Henry kisses his mother's cheek and lopes away from the bed. At the threshold, he turns to look at her, shakes his head, then disappears through the door.

Daniel massages a tic in his right eyelid. "The tedium of the watch," he says finally. Alex looks at him, puzzled.

"You know—'bored with the high drama of watching, I see myself bound always to your absence,' blah, blah, blah, 'imagine, love, the tedium of this watch, on almost every day nothing happens.' Mom makes me read her that poem when she's having a rough time."

Caro shifts in her sleep, sighing as she settles down again.

"A good dream?" Alex asks.

"I think so."

"Then we did the right thing?"

He looks at Caro and then at Alex. "Did we have a choice?"

As if testing his daughter's solidity, as if she too might disappear from him, he squeezes her hand. Then he traces with his thumb the keyhole scar curved along his daughter's eyebrow. He pretends his finger is a key, presses the tip lightly into the scar, and turns it.

"Remember the keys?" he asks.

"The keys? You mean the ones I had when I was little?"

"The very ones." Each key had a story Alex borrowed from fairy tales. A tiny brass key that opened the door to the Queen's rose-garden. A bronze key that released Rapunzel from her lonely tower. A wrought-iron key that last turned the rusty lock of a pirate's swinging gibbet. "Whatever happened to those keys?"

"Jesus, Dad, who cares? That was years ago."

"Not *so* long ago." He frowns, exaggerating the expression so that his lower lip juts out beyond his upper lip.

"Sometimes you're so weird." But before he can say anything else, she leaves the room, disappearing as if through a revolving door and reemerging as her thirteen-year-old self. She's running late for school, she's dawdled over breakfast, her mother has admonished her more than once.

—The bus will be here any minute, and change that shirt, young lady, he hears Caro yell from the bottom of the stairs. He's shaving.

—Daddy, Alex says, pirouetting in a pink camisole top that barely covers her new breasts, how does this look?

He has an absurd thought—she will be a nun. Forget the fact they were Presbyterian. How hard would it be to finagle a vocation to a dying profession, his daughter prostrate before the altar, he vouching for her virginity? Even better, a cloistered nun. There was a movie (was there not?)

where the nuns spent their lives behind wrought-iron bars. Like them, Alex could pass her whole life meditating on the wounds of Christ, or whatever it was those nuns did.

And in the next breath, the very next it seems to him, did it matter what he thought of her skimpy outfits? She became enamored of a different key, a very real key, the black and silver key to the family's aging white Volvo.

The Marshmallow, his kids called it, frankly dismissive of its solid metal cage.

One morning he's shaving again when he gets the call he's anticipated for seventeen years. There's been an accident, your daughter's hurt. He wipes the shaving cream from his face, throws on some clothes, and, because Caro is out driving Henry to school, he races alone to Bryn Mawr Hospital. Alex is alive, of course she's alive, alive alive, laid out on a gurney, blood oozing from a long gash in her forehead but alive, he can see her aliveness in the brown-black of her open eyes.

He forgets giving permission for treatment and the doctor stitching the wound and the words he babbled to ease her pain. But he remembers afterward, holding her head against his chest, and the warmth of her breath through his thin tee-shirt. Then she pulled away and asked, "What happened to your face?"

He ran his hand along his jowl—half-smooth, half-rough, a dab of shaving cream by his left ear. He touches his left ear now, half-expecting to find that same dollop of cream almost three years later. Instead he discovers his beard is rough; he forgets when he last shaved.

"Here we are." Caro comes through the bedroom door, nineteen again, jangling a brass ring of skeleton keys. He blinks. Alex comes through the bedroom door, nineteen again, jangling a brass ring of skeleton keys. She throws them on the bed and says, "They're all yours."

He fingers the pattern of each key, the large ones and the small. "I found the lost key to Snow White's glass coffin, you know."

"The key to what?" She touches his forehead, pretending to check if he is feverish. "Are you all right, Dad?"

"Don't be fresh," he says, and removes her hand. "Surely you remember the accident?"

"I'd rather forget the accident. And just for the record, it wasn't my fault." She touches the scar on her forehead. "What does that have to do with my keys anyway?"

"Not *keys*. Key. Snow White's key," he says. "I went back to the intersection that afternoon. The cars were gone and all that was left of the Volvo was glass." Against the black macadam, in the fall of early evening sunlight, the glass pebbles again sparkle. Yes, he has played with glass, its dual properties of strength and transparency, beauty and nothingness. He sifts the pebbles through his fingers. From these pebbles great buildings grew, buildings composed of sheets of glass through which light fell, divided, fell again. In a stoneless world he would have been a visionary architect. He pockets a handful of glass to show Caro, as if he needs proof of something. His diligence? The vehicle's fragility? The endless possibilities of glass?

"Earth to Dad," she says, "come in Dad."

"Snow White's key was there, beneath the pile of glass. It must have been lost in that car all along."

"That's it? That's the story?"

"What were the chances of finding it there?"

"A miracle to find something so small in a terrain so vast," Caro says, her eyes closed.

"Mom? Mom?" Alex touches her mother's shoulder. "Mom?"

"She does that a lot. I think she hears us even when we're whispering like this, sort of half-understands us but can't quite wake up."

"Mom?"

He rises from the bed, crosses to his bureau, and searches through the watches and old cuff links, francs and lire and loose buttons he keeps in a bowl. "All that time, the key was lost. How long was it? Seven years? Eight? I could swear I told you about the key that night. At least I thought I did..."

"*Mom?*"

"Ah, here it is." He turns back to her, holding up a small gold key and the brass key ring side by side and grinning broadly, as if he has just won a stuffed elephant for her at the school fair. "A miracle, huh?"

"Do you think I care about that damned key? This is all making you stupid, Dad!"

"Stupid? Stupid?" He makes a fist, the brass ring dangling down from his folded knuckles, and thrusts the small gold key into the hole his fist makes. He twists the key back and forth, and though it cuts into his palm, he does not feel pain. "This key," he says, brandishing it in the air between them, surprised he has cut deeply enough to bloody it, "this key made me believe something. Do you know what that thing was?"

"Stop shouting at me!"

"I'm not shouting. This key, this *stupid* key made me believe nothing is lost forever. It's a lie, Alex. Some things are lost. You think you found them, and then there's always one more thing, and one more thing beneath that, the thing you can't reach, the thing you'll never reach even though it's right there, right there, only you can't see it and you'll never see it and it doesn't even matter if you don't see it and what the hell am I even talking about?"

"Stop, stop," Caro moans in her sleep.

Alex opens her mouth to speak, then closes it and shakes her head.

He sits down heavily on the bed. "Alex, honey, I'm sorry," he whispers. "If that makes me stupid, then we're all stupid. Maybe it's better to be stupid."

He tries to secure the little gold key on the ring, but his hands are trembling, and the simple mechanism has suddenly taken on the complexity of the lock the key was meant to open. "I think I'm losing my mind."

Alex takes the key and the ring from him and slides the key along the circle of the metal clasp. Then she rummages on the nightstand, finds an alcohol swab, and tears open the packet. Wiping the blood from his palm, she says, "I'm sorry, too."

He grabs her hands and pulls them around his neck, to comfort her, he thinks, until he realizes that the only tears are his.

"Dad," she says.

"Yes," he says. She is holding his head against her breast, her free hand draped loosely behind his neck, and he is thinking of years ago.

"We did the right thing."

31

Caro kneels on the ground, carving a narrow, oblong figure in the earth and clearing away sod and roots and stones within the oval. It is the very spot where she discovered the bones, under the weeping willow beside the nameless creek. The bones lie in two clear plastic cases beside the figure. Where did they come from? The last time she had seen them, they were in the drawer labeled 1East/4South, laid down and forgotten with the rest of the bones and the pipes and the fire-split rock. A shadow darkens the earth where she works.

—The dead do not stay dead, eh, Dietrich?

—So it seems. He stands over her as she

smoothes the dirt with the triangular blade of her trowel. —You never were one to listen.

—I listened. Then I stopped listening.

—I never saw a woman with your persistence.

She pauses and turns to Dietrich. He is a skeleton with very little flesh, and the blue jeans and white shirt from the church now hang from his gaunt frame. She is not surprised by his appearance; he has been dead for twenty years.

—You've looked better, she says.

He holds out his arms in front of him, examines them as if only noticing for the first time that he is dead.

—Your bone tool turned out to be just a bone broken naturally, not fashioned by human agency, she says. —It wasn't a rude awl or a crude knife, not even a pretty flute. Just a piece of a mammoth's leg bone.

—How can the others prove anything? It's just jealousy, professional fratricide. Nothing like it had ever been found. The spiral fractures, the polish. It had to be made by man.

—The movement of glaciers over the site? A bone broken in a fall?

She turns back to her work and lays four live coals on the mellowed earth inside the oblong figure, eight more around the outside. Her hands burn, the coals singe her skin. The burning is the least of her pain. Pain is pain, no more, no less.

—Maybe a predator slashed the bone with its claws?

—You've made your point, Caroline.

On top of the coals she lays sweet wheatgrass, which smolders then sweeps into flame, a column of red cinders and gray smoke drawn up through the willow branches. The sky has turned the color of liquid mercury. She must hurry; it is going to rain. She cuts a second, smaller oblong behind the first, digs a shallow hole there, and opens the plastic cubes.

—Come, Dietrich, bow your head.

She waits for him to comply; he shrugs, then obeys. She lays the three bones down, the thumb and skull bones cupped inside the pelvis, and covers them with dirt.

—The spirit will never cease to be, she prays. —Never the time when it was not. End and beginning are dreams. Birthless and deathless and changeless remains the spirit forever. Death has not touched it at all, dead though the house of it seems. Amen.

Dietrich raises his head and waves his hand over the burial ground. Every stone, every twig, remains exactly as she has placed it. —I presume there is a certain twisted logic to all this.

—The only logic is that they belong here, she says without taking her eyes from the burial mound. Layering the grave with sprays of artemisia, she whispers, —Your souls are free to depart.

She turns to face Dietrich, touching his sullen, skeletal face. —If it's a comfort, no one's proven anything definitively. Someone someday will happen upon a cave in Virginia or a rockshelter in the Smokies. No doubt they'll be arguing long after we're dead.

She strokes his cheek. His face fleshes out, beautiful and dangerous, her heart is racing, she's twenty-two. What if she stays? He is her adventure, her ache for endless distance. She is his convenient virgin. Oh, she is capable, too. They found Clovis. Measured against all she had found with Daniel, that is nothing.

—I stole your amber relic, you know. She holds up her hand, and Dietrich's stone appears, the amber with the tiny insect trapped inside.

—I suspected as much, he says, moving toward her.

—You're not angry?

He grabs her wrist. —I'm still angry.

Pain, pain, pain. He is squeezing the life from her. The stone falls and shatters against the hard ground into rays of amber light.

—Let go of me.

—Why, Caroline? He releases her arm, kneels in the pile of tiny pebbles, and picks up a handful of light. —I let you go.

He looks up at her. She is tall, as tall as the sun, and he is shrinking into the pool of liquid amber. —You're wrong, Dietrich. You never had me.

His flesh turns to bone, his skeleton to dust, and Daniel is kneeling there, caught in the hardening amber. She scrapes away layer after layer to release him, but in her haste, she goes too far. His skin peels away. She sees the pattern of his bones, his silent, beaten heart.

She touches his heart. "A miracle to find something so small in terrain so vast."

"*Mom?*" Alex's voice cuts through the dream. And then she hears Daniel crying, far away and nearby he is crying and Alex is soothing him, but she cannot see him and she cannot go to him, and who knows? Her husband's sadness might also be a dream.

32

The mother coyote peers from her outcropping in the rock. It is fall. The wheatgrass is tall, gilded by mid-autumn sun, and hunch-backed bison only pepper the grass where they used to blot out the landscape, and a few wild horses paint black streaks against a violent blue sky. At the entrance to the den, a young female coyote paces, her wheaten hair singed with a ridge of black along the back of her lean torso. She alone among her sisters has survived the wolves and the mountain lions, the spring blizzard, the summer drought. Her dark-eyed brother nudges his mother's flank with his nose. The mother nuzzles his copper-colored fur, and then pushes him from behind across the threshold.

He leaves, glancing back only once. The brother and sister strike out together for the white hills. They have been taught to do this, to hunt for prey in tandem, to rely on the keenness of their hunger, their desire. Behind them, their mother howls, a single long note rising then falling, impossible to fix exactly in one place. The sky tears along its blue seam. The wind is warm and cold, warm and cold, and Caro is floating beside the girl and the boy, past the bison and the wild horses, over the white hills, across the bad lands they must cross. There is paradise in this danger the boy marks with the scent of his urine, fixing a territory with no beginning and no end. They are lost. They pause, prick up their ears, listen for their mother's howl. All is silence, and the wind.

33

Sunlight and shadow cut a path before them.

They are alone, huddled together under the covers, sleeping in the sunlight that seeps through the branches of the giant sycamore and falls through their bedroom window. The tracery of the branches, the twining of dark leaves, and the tiny silhouettes of the jays imprint their shadows on the beige carpet, stretch and lengthen across the white coverlet that warms the couple sleeping underneath. The shadows of late morning, a late morning years ago or now. The couple remembers the mornings of time suspended by sunlight and shadow and sex, they remember the now.

"*Haŋ le miye što*, Alex," the wife mumbles to the daughter walking beside her.

"Hand me stone," the husband echoes, and strokes his wife's shoulder in his sleep.

They fell asleep together, they do not remember when, and the husband does not want to wake, but instead walk down this path they have created together, fashioned simply of sunlight and shadow.

"Little Magpie, Mother's here," the wife calls to her son, who is walking just ahead of her. The mother does not want to lose sight of him.

"Time to sleep," the man mutters, the sun a drug that will not let him wake.

"I want to go. I want to stay."

"There were things I wanted, too," the man says, and gathers his wife in his arms, letting the children run ahead of them.

34

Her lips form the single word "want." She wants the children to come back.

Daniel wakes to her want. They were in a dream together. He could feel her beside him, not his dream Caro but the real one.

"Sweetheart, are you awake?"

"The child not knowing her mother was dead still nursed." She catches the scent of pine and what rises beneath the pine, the odor of unwashed bodies, the metallic smell of blood. The silent night has turned to morning, and the notes that rise are those from the shuffle of the sycamore against the window screen and the jays calling to each other across the green lawn. The child lets go the mother's nipple and turns to Caro, who moans softly.

Daniel fingers the top of her spine and the hard knot that gives her so much pain. He circles the knot with his thumb, gently, willing the pain to go away. "'Imagine you could have seen that side of me at the beginning...'"

"'When we walked for hours,' and, and...," she says, wincing.

"'You were so certain I was'—"

"It's not working. Press there. Harder. There."

"You are awake, then." He pushes his palm into the knot and holds it there. They can feel the heat the lump creates in the friction of cells multiplying out of control. "We were walking together."

"Yes, walking."

He continues to knead the top of her spine, wondering how it is possible to share the same dream. "Better?"

"A little." She kisses his hand. They both know the pain is exactly the same. "I don't think it'll be long."

"Don't talk like that. You're shivering. Would you like another blanket?"

"It's dark here," she says, though she is bathed in as much sunlight as shadow. "Hold me."

He takes her in his arms, his chin resting on the top of her head. His body easily envelops hers, her heels touching his ankles, her cheek nestled against his bare chest. They had been surprised, the first time they held each other, to find their long bodies fit together so perfectly. His heart beats clearly, steadily, in the whorls of her ear. Not his heart, but the echo of his heart, the pulse of his blood.

"I'm in a cave, I think. It looks like a cave. It must have been at the end of the path."

"We were walking—"

"Yes, walking—"

"With the children?"

She nods, kisses the bottom of his chin. Somewhere out ahead of her, there is a woman she does not recognize.

—Have you ever seen, the strange woman asks, so many wonderful rich colors? The woman turns to her, smiling, a peculiar light on her head.

"The black cow is falling. It's a strange word, fall. So many shades of meaning."

"Where are you, Caro?"

"Where you are is where I am."

He shakes his head. "I mean which cave?"

"Falling, fell, the fall. We spend our lives falling. Adam and Eve fell. Bodies fall, one into another. Ashes to ashes, we all fall down. Henry is falling, but he has wings. The wings catch his fall."

"Is he an egg?"

"What?"

At least they had not shared that particular nightmare, he thinks. "I'm kidding, sweetheart."

"Did I just say Henry has wings? I'm sorry, Daniel. Nothing I say makes sense, does it?"

"You'd be surprised how much sense you're making."

The woman waves Caro ahead of her, the uncertain light of her lamp casting shadows on the path, and she is suddenly alone in the Great Hall of the Bulls. She opens her eyes. "The caves at Lascaux," she says. "That's where I am. It wasn't our Henry with wings. It was the stick man with the bird's head, remember? Do you think even 15,000 years ago men dreamed of flying?"

"Men have dreamed it for as long as there's been air." He sifts his fingers through the gray down on her temple and smiles. "Of course, there's also Daedalus."

"Poor Icarus." His hand on her scalp warms both, making them forget, for the moment, the burning in her bones. "I would've liked to see the unicorn again."

"I'll take the kids. I'll say to them, 'Mom and I planned to come here again before she got sick.'"

She places her hands on his shoulders and looks straight at him. "It will be different without me."

"Yes."

She notices then the bruise on his ribcage, a blueblack circle swathed with blood blistering beneath the surface. She traces its edges in the hills and valleys of his ribs. "Where did this come from?"

He touches the rib where she elbowed him in the night, the soreness still making it hard for him to draw a deep breath. "This? This is nothing." He rubs her arms. "You're shivering again."

"I can't seem to stay warm."

He gets up to retrieve a blanket from the dresser, fans the blanket over the bed, and then climbs in behind her, cupping his body around hers. Her shivering quiets a little. Nothing stirs, nothing moves, except for their breathing together.

She reaches back and touches his thigh. "Someone will find Eden. We didn't dig deep enough, or we were looking in the wrong place all along."

"In the Badlands?"

"*Ces mauvaises terres que je dois traverser.*"

"Something you forgot? Something more that happened?"

"It's still happening—the hemione butting heads with the horse, the unicorn chasing the aurochs."

She turns to face him, her eyes searching his. "Bury me in the blue dress. And mother's pearls. Tell Alex to take care of Henry. And tell Henry not to bite his nails. Tell him I said so as my dying wish."

"You'll not die just yet."

She presses her forehead into his. "Where are the kids?"

"Alex dragged Henry out of bed to go grocery shopping. Last I saw them they were arguing about who should drive because—"

"Did you know our breath could extinguish them?"

"The children?"

"No, the paintings. Weren't we talking about Lascaux? Human breath erodes the paint or harms the rock's surface or something. I can't remember exactly."

"All of that, I think."

"We weren't meant to see the paintings. Ever. It was an accident. The bull gives birth to the bear. Or is it the other way around? What were we talking about? Is any of this making sense?"

"Perfect sense." He leans his head away from hers and grasps her chin. "We're at Lascaux, looking at the painting of the bear hidden inside the bull. No one knows what it means. It could be the evolution of one creature from another. It could be—"

"Chance. Simple chance."

The staccato of falling books, dust rising through the carrels, her face hovering over his. *Are you all right?* He takes her hand.

"Bury me in the white sea."

"Caro—"

"You have always been, and before you nothing," she whispers. "Do you remember when Little Magpie was stung by the yellow-jackets?"

"Henry, you mean. He was pretending to be an Indian. I've never seen you so angry."

"He had no idea what he was doing." She sounds angry even now.

"It was only a boy's game. *I* used to play cowboys and Indians, for heaven's sake." He is holding her tight to his chest, the warmth of their bodies warming each other. "He should have been wearing shoes. Didn't I always tell him to wear shoes?"

"Oh, *Mother*," she laughs. "Don't you think the pain was enough punishment? And the swelling afterwards? He never went barefoot again."

"A hard lesson."

"This one will be harder." She tries to swallow the phlegm clogging her throat. "Nothing is working. It's not working. I don't want to drift away. I'm drifting, Daniel." Suddenly she turns still, limp in his arms.

"Sweetheart?" He lets go of her body and cradles her face in his hands. Her eyes are closed. "Caro?"

"Do the footprints dance still?" she asks. "Do the dead lie dead in the white sea?"

"Not yet," he says. "I'm not ready."

"Don't worry." Her eyes flutter open. "The dead do not stay dead."

"I'm counting on it."

"Ours was a beautiful dream, Daniel. I need to go home."

"You are home. This is your home." His eyes begin to water. "'Imagine, love, the tedium of this watch…'"

"'On almost every day nothing happens.'" She laughs, wipes the tears from his eyes. "This is the long now. Don't you see, Daniel? Everything's still happening, everything at once."

In the library, a book begins to fall. In the delivery room, a baby takes its first breath. A chair crashes into a table. Wild laughter. A bracelet slides from the wrist, a pipe breaks in two, stone falls against stone. A creek freezes over, a mastodon crushes a mammoth's bone, yellow-jackets buzz and hover, snow falls, a song rises, a single note echoes, the bison return, thundering over the ridge in a snowstorm.

"This far north, the earth curves away from you. This far north, everything is white...oh, Daniel, how *does* one speak to the dead?"

"I suppose you could start by saying hello."

She closes her eyes and whispers, "Hello."

Acknowledgments

I am deeply indebted to the many people who were instrumental in helping to shape this book; to the sources used in the research of Wounded Knee, archaeology, glass architecture, and Lakota language, stories, and rituals; and to the poets and writers whose work enriched this story.

Voices of Wounded Knee by William S. E. Coleman was a crucial source for historical testimony about the Wounded Knee Massacre. Coleman's narrative is unique in that it tells the story of Wounded Knee by piecing together the accounts of many participants and witnesses and often juxtaposing contradictory versions of the same events. This book consolidated in a single volume thirty years of Coleman's research: much of its primary source material would otherwise have been unavailable to me. I am grateful to the University of Nebraska Press for permitting me to use the Lakota words to one of the Ghost Dance songs transcribed by Coleman during a private interview with Ben Black Elk, son of Black Elk. I also first discovered here the historical testimony contained in the Gilmore epigraph, many of the fragments in the stream of voices in Chapter 4, and the Forsyth and Beard quotes in Chapter 13.

The West by Geoffrey Ward provided a larger historical context in which to frame the events leading to Wounded Knee, and a perspective on the massacre itself. Excerpts from the English translation of the two Ghost Dance songs, Little Magpie's story of the Ghost Dance in Chapter 13, and details about a bullet passing through a braid and boys playing leap frog and bucking horse before the massacre came from this book.

Among the many other books I consulted for additional information on the massacre and the history of North American Indians were *The Last Days of the Sioux Nation* (Second Edition) by Robert M. Utley, *Trail to Wounded Knee: The Last Stand of the Plains Indians* by Herman J. Viola, and *500 Nations* by Alvin M. Josephy, Jr.

For background on archaeology and the first Americans, the following proved invaluable: *A Brief History of Archaeology*, *Ancient North America: The Archaeology of a Continent* (Third Edition), and *The Great Journey: The Peopling of Ancient America*, all by Brian M. Fagan; *The First Americans: In Pursuit of Archaeology's Greatest Mystery* by J. M. Adovasio; *Beginner's Guide to Archaeology* by Louis A. Brennan; *The Bone Hunters: The Heroic Age of Paleontology in the American West* by Url Lanham; and *Digging Up Bones* by D. R. Brothwell. *NOVA's* program "America's Stone Age Explorers" helped clarify the controversy surrounding the peopling of the Americas.

I discovered Lascaux in a children's book called *Painters of the Great Caves* by Patricia Lauber. *Paintings that Changed the World* by Klaus Reichold and Bernhard Graf provided additional information.

For background on Taut and glass architecture, *Bruno Taut: Alpine Architektur* by Matthias Schirren was a key resource.

The essay "The American West and the Burden of Belief" in *The Man Made of Words* by N. Scott Momaday offered insights on the nature of language and the differences between its oral and written traditions, as well as on the Wounded Knee Massacre. It is the source of the line "language bears the burden of the sacred." *Lakota Dictionary*, compiled and edited by Eugene Buechel and Paul Manhart, was an indispensable reference for reading and writing in the Lakota language. Background on Lakota wisdom and rituals was found in *Lakota Belief and Ritual* by James R. Walker and *The Lakota Way* by Joseph M. Marshall III.

For Native American folklore, I consulted a

number of sources, including *American Indian Myths and Legends*, selected and edited by Richard Erdoes and Alfonso Ortiz, *Native American Stories* by Joseph Bruchac, and a lovely children's book by Paul Goble entitled *The Legend of the White Buffalo Woman*. The story of Thunder-Bird was adapted from "Why Gartersnake Wears a Green Blanket," found in *Coyote Stories* by Mourning Dove and used by permission of University of Nebraska Press.

I also extend my gratitude to the poets and writers whose words appear in these pages. Lawrence Raab's remarkable poem "'My Soul Is a Light Housekeeper,'" which I first read in *The New Yorker* (September 19, 1994) and rediscovered in his book *The Probable World*, helped to open up a draft of a closed story that became this novella. I am also indebted to Wallace Stevens for "Sunday Morning" (from *The Collected Poems of Wallace Stevens*); T. S. Eliot for "The Love Song of J. Alfred Prufrock" (from *T. S. Eliot: The Complete Poems and Plays 1909-1950*); Roald Dahl for his wonderful memoirs; Alfred, Lord Tennyson for "Break, Break, Break" (from *Tennyson: Selected Poetry*); Lewis Carroll for *Alice in Wonderland*; Algernon Charles Swinburne for "The Triumph of Time" (from *The Poems of Algernon Charles Swinburne*); and George Eliot for the inspiration behind Caroline's line "Time rushes past, and we see nothing but sand; angels visit us, but we only know them when they're gone."

Any factual errors contained in *Badlands* are my responsibility.

I would also like to thank the following people for their support and guidance in the preparation of this book: my teachers at Warren Wilson's MFA Program, especially Michael Martone, Kevin McIlvoy, and C. J. Hribal; Miami University Press, especially Margaret Luongo, Dana Leonard, Keith Tuma, and the design staff; Henry C. Smith III, for his help with Lakota Sioux rituals and language, and his meticulous readings of the final drafts; and my friends, especially Catherine Brown, for her careful eye, Pete and Nancy Mondozzi, for their continual encouragement, and Beth Proffitt, for the carved white buffalo talisman. Special thanks to my family, Douglas, Elizabeth, and Christopher Reeves, for their patience and endless attention to detail.

Questions & Topics for Discussion

1. *Badlands* fuses a strong narrative line—propelled by a night of crisis brought on by the uncontrollable pain Caro experiences as she is dying—with a hybrid of collage and other forms of juxtaposition that fracture time and mirror the psychological states of Caro and her husband, Daniel. In what ways is this experience of reading different than reading a temporally linear narrative?

2. It is clear from the beginning of the novella that Caro will die. Given that this outcome is assured, how does the novella create and sustain tension? How do the individual components of the story shape the arc of the story as a whole?

3. At twenty-two, Daniel is captivated by the

crystalline buildings of the visionary German architect Bruno Taut, but Caro is horrified at the idea of transparency, that is, exposing private lives to public view. How is transparency explored in *Badlands*? What images are used to develop this idea? In what ways does marriage as an institution subject spouses to the kind of transparency Caro reacts against?

4. *Badlands* shifts between the points of view of Daniel and Caro. Several times in the novella, the same incident is told from their different perspectives, for example, the family story of their son Henry being stung by yellow-jackets. How does screening events from two different points of view influence the reader's understanding of those events?

5. When Caro tells Henry the Sioux story of the white buffalo woman, she is trying to pass on knowledge that is part of her, to preserve herself in her son's memory. In what other ways does this novella attempt to address the idea of story-telling and its power to shape memory? In what ways do the stories within stories contribute to the novella's overall effect?

6. During their long relationship, Daniel and Caro have argued about "finding order and meaning in the chaos of conflicting truths while recognizing in advance that one is attempting something fundamentally impossible." Caro recognizes that stories take on new meaning as details are added or as new evidence is

uncovered, but that this does not invalidate the process of discovery. In what ways does the novella address this limitation of perception?

7. *Badlands* weaves together multiple experiences of time, even to the extent that at certain points, everything seems to happen at once. Early in the novella, for example, several events run together in Daniel's mind as he drifts in and out of sleep: the present, that is, sleeping next to Caro, and three events from the past, their wedding night (when she was ill), the night one week later when they consummated their marriage, and the night two years ago when he first made love to her after the mastectomy. What does it mean for time to run together for Daniel in this way? In what ways does time compress and distort for the other characters? How do the elasticity of time and the fluidity of memory contribute to the novella's overall effect?

8. Caro's experience of Sioux ritual, language, and history is filtered through her own understanding of that culture and also through her altered consciousness. How does a writer outside of a particular culture or ethnicity write about the experience from a position of empathy without presuming to fully grasp the nuances of experience of that culture?

9. In the closing chapters, Daniel and Caro seem at times to share the same consciousness. In what ways has the novella been building to

this moment? How is the effect of shared consciousness achieved?

10. The epigraph of the book contains two fragments: part of Lawrence Raab's poem "'My Soul Is a Light Housekeeper'" and an excerpt from historical testimony of Dr. Melvin R. Gilmore regarding survivors at Wounded Knee who later perished in obscurity. How do these two seemingly disparate fragments function in relation to each other and in the larger context of the work?

About the Author

Cynthia Reeves is a native of the Philadelphia area and lives with her husband and two children near Valley Forge, Pennsylvania. Her fiction and poetry have appeared in a number of journals and anthologies, including *Crab Orchard Review*, *Ontario Review*, and *Wreckage of Reason: Anthology of XXperimental Women Writers Writing in the 21st Century*. She is currently at work on a novel in stories set in post-World War I Italy, three of which have been published in *Colorado Review*, *Silk Road*, and *Words+Images 2007*. She holds an MFA in Creative Writing from Warren Wilson College. *Badlands* is her first book.